*Somebody Go
and Bang a Drum*

illustrated by Jack Hearne

Somebody Go
and Bang a Drum

by Rebecca Caudill

E. P. DUTTON & CO., INC.   NEW YORK

LIBRARY OF CONGRESS CATALOGING IN PUBLICATION DATA

Caudill, Rebecca.   Somebody go and bang a drum.

SUMMARY: A couple with one child adopts seven others of
varying nationalities and races.

[1. Family life—Fiction.   2. Brotherliness—Fiction]
I. Hearne, Jack, illus.   II. Title.
PZ7.C274So   [Fic]   73-13809   ISBN 0-525-39575-x

Published simultaneously in Canada by Clarke,
Irwin & Company Limited, Toronto and Vancouver

Designed by Riki Levinson
Printed in the U.S.A.   First Edition

To
the Father and the Mother
of the Children
with ever-deepening admiration
and affection

Contents

1 / Along Came Eric   1

2 / Then Ginny   11

3 / And Angela   29

4 / And Gene   46

5 / And Mark   61

6 / And Julie   79

7 / And Peter   95

8 / And, Finally, Emily   107

1

Along Came Eric

The children live in a city in North Carolina, on a street named Hemlock Drive. There are eight of them, four boys and four girls. They are yellow and brown and black and white, and they are brothers and sisters.

Even when the children aren't playing in the yard, you can easily find their house. It is the only green house on the block, and it is set in a big yard with many trees back of it.

In the springtime and summer, if you go by, you might see Eric or Mark mowing the lawn in front of the house or on either side of it. If you walk around the house to the big backyard, you might find Julie and Emily, and maybe even Angela, playing with their dolls in the tree house their father built for them high up in a giant oak tree. Not far from the giant oak is a smaller oak. From its lowest branch hangs a stout rope swing. Here you might see Ginny or Gene swinging Emily or Peter.

Back of the trees is a wild place through which a small creek gurgles its way to the river below. On its banks in the springtime, jacks-in-the-pulpit and violets and spring beauties grow among the willows and alders that line the stream. Minnows dart about in the sparkling water. Crawfishes scuttle backward and hide under the stones, and, very early in the spring, frogs come out of their mud houses at the bottom of the creek and croak among the reeds along the banks.

The frogs, with their croaking, often tempt Mark and Gene to go in hot chase after them, and Peter to go in hot chase after Mark and Gene.

But this is getting ahead of the story.

The story begins in a big city in Texas. It begins with Edie, the mother of the children, and with Julian, their father. It begins before any of the children were born.

Edie was a social worker. She worked at Neighborhood House. For many blocks around Neighborhood House lived people who were part Mexican and part American.

In most Mexican-American homes, there were many children. After school and on Saturdays the children came to Neighborhood House where Edie played games with them, took them on trips about the city, told them stories, and helped them put on plays. Sometimes she took them by bus to a big city park. Once she took them to a puppet show. Later she helped them make puppets and put on puppet shows of their own.

On Friday evenings, Mexican-American boys and girls of high school age came to Neighborhood House. There they played records on an old record player and danced.

Edie danced with them. They taught her Mexican-American dances, and she taught them square dances she had learned in her home in Indiana.

One morning when Edie was eating her breakfast, she turned on the radio and heard a voice that was new to her. It was the voice of a young man broadcasting the news, and it was deep and clear and strong.

Edie liked the voice. She wondered who the young man was. Soon, quite by accident, she met him. His name was Julian Garth.

Julian liked broadcasting the news. He discovered that he liked Neighborhood House, too. He especially liked Mexican-American children. In his free time he began helping Edie. He helped her with the dances on Friday evenings. Sometimes he helped her take the children on trips.

And then, something happened. Julian and Edie fell in love. Before long they were married. They were very happy. And they went on with their work, Edie at Neighborhood House, Julian at the radio station, broadcasting the news.

One day Julian came hurrying home from the radio station with a letter to show to Edie. It had come from a university in Illinois. Would Julian come to the university in the fall, the letter asked, and teach some classes in broadcasting while he studied for a degree in radio and television?

Edie read the letter through. She read it again.

"It's just what you want to do, isn't it?" she asked. "And of course you must go. But I'll have one regret."

"What's that?" asked Julian.

"It will be awfully hard to leave these children," Edie

told him. "I've come to think of them almost as our own."

"I know," said Julian. "But wherever you go, Edie, there'll be children needing you."

In the early fall, just before the opening of school, Julian and Edie moved to Illinois. First of all, they went hunting for an apartment. They found one—a tiny one— they thought must have been made just for them. It was built over a garage at the end of a long, tree-shaded drive-way. Its windows opened out onto a world of green leaves and birdsong. When Edie and Julian went to bed there the first night, they lay awake and listened to the chirping of crickets, the purring of tree toads, and the sound of the lively wind.

"I feel as if I'm sleeping in a bird's nest," said Edie.

"It lacks one thing," said Julian.

"What's that?"

"A baby."

Edie lay quietly for a moment. "Where in the world would we put a baby in this tiny nest?" she asked.

"In a corner," said Julian.

"How many babies shall we have?" asked Edie.

"Oh," said Julian, "about four."

"Quadruplets?" asked Edie. "One for each corner?"

Julian laughed. "One at a time, please!" he said. "And," he added, "do you know something I've been thinking?"

"I couldn't begin to guess," said Edie.

"I know how sorry you felt to leave those children in Texas," Julian told her. "So why don't we have two children of our own? Just two. The earth is going to be awfully crowded,'' he added, ''if parents keep on having big families. After we've had two children of our own, we can adopt two Mexican-American children. There are plenty of them who are orphans needing a home.''

So it was agreed.

The next day Julian went to classes at the university, and Edie went looking for a job in town. Soon she found a job with a social agency. She found that, just as Julian had said, there were plenty of children needing help—black children and white children, and children part black and part white. But there were no Mexican-American children.

As Julian studied and taught university classes, Edie worked with the children. She and Julian were very happy in their bird nest. They were happiest of all because a baby was growing inside Edie, their very own, their first.

As the weeks passed, Edie and Julian made plans to welcome the baby. They bought a baby bed from a second-hand store. Julian mended it, and Edie painted it yellow. She shopped for nighties and shirts and diapers and safety pins and all the other things babies need.

More weeks passed. The waiting seemed very long.

''We don't have a name for the baby,'' Julian reminded Edie one night.

They tried out boys' names. William. Thomas. Henry. James. Arthur. Eric. And they tried out girls' names, just in case. Mary. Beulah. Anna. Augusta. Virginia.

''Do you know which name I like best?'' asked Julian. ''Eric.''

''All right,'' agreed Edie. ''Eric it will be—unless it's Virginia.''

At last the day came. Julian hurried Edie to the hospital,

and there, in the delivery room, the baby was born, a little boy baby: Eric. Eric Dana Garth.

When Edie was back in her hospital room, a nurse brought Eric for her and Julian to see. Edie turned back the soft blanket from around the baby's face and looked lovingly at him.

"Isn't he beautiful!" exclaimed Julian as he bent over the baby.

Edie began to laugh. "I've always imagined we'd have the most beautiful baby in the world," she said, "but we'll have to be honest, Julian. He—he's lots of things. But he isn't beautiful."

Eric screwed up his wrinkled, red face and yawned.

Julian bent over him again. "He does look like a dried-up apple, doesn't he?" he admitted.

Every evening while Edie and Eric were in the hospital Julian hurried to see them. Late one night, in their tiny apartment, he printed announcements of Eric's birth on a small printing press borrowed from a friend. The words he printed were written by a great poet of India.

> *Every child comes with the message that*
> *God is not yet discouraged of man.*
> *—Rabindranath Tagore*

ERIC DANA GARTH

was born June 21, 1958, at 5:27 P.M.
Weight 7 pounds ½ ounce

Julian mailed the announcements to their relatives and friends. He mailed one to Neighborhood House in Texas so that everyone there would know about Eric. The children especially would be happy with the news, he thought to himself, as he dropped the announcement in the post box.

The day Edie came home from the hospital, she and Julian had hardly settled Eric in his crib before they heard a loud knocking at their front door.

When Julian opened the door, there stood Grandma and Grandpa Anderson.

"Why, Mother! And Dad!" exclaimed Edie. "We weren't expecting you! You came all the way from Indiana this afternoon?"

"We couldn't take time to let you know," said Grandma. "As soon as we got word from Julian that you'd be home today, we just threw a few things in the car, shut the house door, and set out."

"Where's that boy?" demanded Grandpa.

Edie hurried to the crib in a corner of the room and lifted Eric to her shoulder for them to see.

"Oh!" sighed Grandma. "Isn't he a beautiful, beautiful baby!"

"Looks like me, don't you think, Ma?" Grandpa Anderson asked proudly of Grandma.

Grandma Anderson handed Edie a package wrapped in blue paper and gaily tied with blue ribbons.

Edie unwrapped the package. Inside lay a book of poetry.

"Thank you, Mother," she said. "It will be quite a while before Eric is ready for that," she added, laughing.

"Oh," said Grandma, tossing her head knowingly, "maybe not so long as you think."

Grandpa was holding two envelopes in his hand. "Here," he said, handing them to Edie. "These were in your mailbox."

Edie looked at the envelopes. Both had come from old friends. She opened one and together she and Julian read the message inside. It quoted an old American Indian chant celebrating the birth of a baby. It began:

> "Ho! Ye Sun, Moon, Stars,
> all ye that move in the heavens,
> I bid you hear me!
> Into your midst has come a new life.
> Consent ye, I implore!
> Make its path smooth,
> that it may reach the brow of the first hill."

Edie opened the second envelope. Together she and Julian read:

> "With chortle-ings and glee we prance—
> The family tree has got a branch.
> O joy! O bliss! O rapture blest—
> A little bird is in the nest.
> Somebody go and bang a drum,
> And spread the news the Baby's come!"

2

Then Ginny

From the day he was born, Eric, like all other healthy babies, ate and slept, cried and smiled and grew.

Before he was six months old, he could sit alone. The day he was eight months old, he clutched and tugged and strained at a chair until he pulled himself to his feet.

"Eric sure was proud today when he pulled himself up," Julian said to Edie in the evening as he closed one textbook and reached for another.

"So were you," Edie said without looking up from the magazine she was reading. "Talk about a proud papa! You were it!"

She went on with her reading as Julian, with a smile on his face, went on with his studying.

"Listen to what this magazine says, Julian," Edie said a few minutes later. " 'There are at least thirty thousand

orphaned and abandoned Chinese children in Hong Kong who need a home.' ''

"Thirty thousand!" Julian stared at her. "That's more than all the people in this city."

'' 'They are living in huts or caves, and sleeping on the roofs of houses or in the streets,' '' Edie read. '' 'They have no food to eat, no shelter, no place to go. Most of them are little girls.' ''

Julian put down his book, walked across the room, and read over Edie's shoulder.

"That's grim," he said. "That's really grim."

Together they read, '' 'The adoption of these little girls outside Hong Kong is their only chance for any kind of normal life. Some of them have been adopted by families in the United States. But not nearly enough families have applied for children.' ''

Edie closed the magazine slowly and put it down.

During the week that followed, Eric pulled himself up three or four times a day. Julian grew prouder and prouder.

"I believe it's time to begin reading to him," said Edie.

"Try it this evening," suggested Julian. "I want to see if he listens."

At bedtime, Edie brought the book of poetry Grandma Anderson had given Eric, and, holding the child in her arms, read to him:

> "Someone came knocking at my wee, small door,
> Someone came knocking, I'm sure, sure, sure.
> I listened. I opened. . . ."

As Edie read, Eric lay quiet, listening, listening, and Julian watched.

"That boy's going to like books," he predicted. "Someday, maybe, he's going to be a college professor."

"Can you imagine anyone as gentle as Eric growing up to be a stern college professor?" asked Edie. "Like you? Maybe he'll be a poet."

Together Edie and Julian put Eric to bed.

"You've been so quiet the last few days, Edie," said Julian, sitting down once more beside his books.

"Have I?" asked Edie. "I hadn't realized that."

"What's on your mind?" asked Julian.

"Maybe it's all those Chinese children," answered Edie. "I keep thinking about thirty thousand children with nobody to read to them the way I just read to Eric. Nobody to love them the way we love him."

"You're not thinking about adopting one into the Garth family, are you?" asked Julian.

"Yes," admitted Edie, "I am."

"What about the Mexican-American children we planned to adopt?" asked Julian.

"I never saw a Mexican-American child sleeping on a roof nor in the street," said Edie. "So maybe we ought to change our plans."

"Do you know how to go about adopting a Chinese child?" asked Julian.

"Yes," said Edie. "It's simple. We first ask the social agency here to approve us. A social worker will visit us to see if we live in a suitable home. People at the agency will decide if we would be good parents for an adopted child. They'll ask how much money you make, and they'll decide if we can support another child. That sort of thing."

"And after that?"

"There's a social agency in New York called International Social Service that helps with the adoption of children of all nations. We'd write to the people there, tell them what kind of Chinese child we want, and ask them to find one for us," explained Edie.

"What kind of child do you want?" Julian asked.

"What kind of child do you want?" Edie asked.

"What kind of child do *we* want?" Julian corrected her.

"All right. What kind of child do *we* want? How about a little girl?" asked Edie. "About the same age as Eric. Then they could grow up together."

"I wonder how Eric would accept a Chinese sister?"

"If we love her, he'll love her," said Edie.

"I know a name for her," said Julian. "Remember what we were going to name Eric if he was a girl? Virginia? We'll call her Ginny. Ginny Garth. How do you like the sound of that name?"

"Ginny Garth," Edie repeated. "Fine!"

"What must we do besides ask the social agency here to approve us and write International Social Service?" asked Julian.

"We'll have to buy Ginny's ticket from Hong Kong to Chicago," said Edie.

"From Hong Kong to Chicago!" gasped Julian. "How much is that?"

"The article said about four hundred to four hundred fifty dollars from Hong Kong to Seattle," Edie told him. "Then there'll be the cost of a ticket from Seattle to Chicago. Maybe six hundred dollars altogether."

Julian took his billfold from his pocket and thumbed through it. "We don't have even six dollars," he reported.

"But Ginny won't be leaving right away," Edie reminded him. "While we wait we can save a dollar here and a dollar there. By the time Ginny is ready to come, I'm sure we can save enough money to pay her fare. Anyway," she added, "I don't know anybody who's going to pay it for us."

"And had you thought of this?" Julian asked. "There isn't room for another baby in this bird nest. We'll have to find a bigger apartment."

"We can do that, too," said Edie.

Julian studied her face. He kissed her tenderly. "You do want this child very much, don't you?"

"Yes," admitted Edie. "Yes, I do. I've thought so much about her that she seems real. But," she added, "we must do nothing until we agree on it—until you want her as much as I do."

"Shall we think about it a few days?" suggested Julian. "Though already," he admitted, "I think I'm beginning to believe it would be pretty special having a little daughter in the house."

For a week Edie and Julian thought about and talked about Ginny. They even talked to Eric about her. But Eric was more interested in the poems Edie read to him than he was in Ginny. As Edie and Julian talked, Ginny became real to both of them. Finally, on an afternoon when Julian had no classes, he and Edie and Eric went together to the local social agency where Edie had worked when the Garths first moved to Illinois. They had come, Edie told the social worker, to apply for a little Chinese orphan.

"But, Edie," said the social worker, "you know your-self that few social agencies approve of parents adopting a child of a different race. Why don't you adopt a white American child?"

"But these Chinese children have little chance at life unless American families adopt them," Edie told her. "There are American families willing to adopt most Ameri-can children who need adoption. But few American families are willing to adopt a Chinese child."

"Why don't I talk to the supervisor?" suggested the social worker. "We'll see what she says and let you know later."

A week later the supervisor telephoned Edie. "We have decided it will be all right for you to adopt a Chinese child," she said.

That night Edie wrote to International Social Service. She and Julian wished to adopt a Chinese orphan, she told the director. They wanted a little girl, she wrote, about the age of Eric, not quite a year old.

"I'll take the letter to the post office tonight," said Julian, "so it will get to New York as soon as possible."

Everyday, for weeks after Julian had mailed the letter, Edie hurried to the mailbox as soon as she heard the lid of the box clang. But the postman brought no letter from Inter-national Social Service.

"Maybe our letter got lost in the mail," Edie said to Julian one day. "Do you suppose I ought to write another?"

"Let's wait a little longer," advised Julian. "Maybe it's just as well things don't move along fast. We have to save up those six hundred dollars, you know."

Months later, on a snowy day in January, Edie found in

the mailbox what she and Julian had been waiting for—a
letter from International Social Service. It was short, but it
said everything they wanted it to say: "We will happily
place a child in your home just as soon as we find a child
such as you want."

"That shouldn't be hard," said Julian, "when they
have thirty thousand to choose from."

Days passed. Weeks passed, even months, and during
this time the postman brought no other letter from International Social Service.

While Edie and Julian waited, they found another apartment—a larger one than the bird nest, with an extra bedroom, bright and sunny, and big enough for three baby
beds. The Garths moved into it right away. And in April, on
a Saturday when Julian was home, came another letter from
International Social Service—a fat, bulky one.

"Edie!" shouted Julian excitedly as he hurried into the
apartment waving the letter. "Come see what we've got!"

Edie hurried from the kitchen. "You open it," she said
when she saw the fat envelope. "I'm too excited!"

Julian ripped open the envelope. "Eric!" he called.
"Come find out about your baby sister."

Eric came running on his sturdy legs. The three of them
sat on the sofa while Julian read.

" 'We have found a little orphan girl who we think will
fit beautifully into your home. She is about eighteen months
old.' "

"Two months younger than you, Eric," said Edie.
"Just what we asked for."

" 'She was found by a policeman, abandoned on the
porch of a church,' " Julian read. " 'The policeman took

her to an orphanage for foundlings. The day was October 19, 1958. The people in the orphanage judged her to be two months old, so they gave her a birth date, August 19, 1958. She is very tiny.' ''

"Probably starved," said Edie.

" 'She has just taken her first step or two,' '' Julian read further.

"Too weak to walk," commented Edie.

" 'As soon as a child is placed in an American home, we see that she gets extra food to make her strong enough to take the long trip to America,' '' Julian continued his reading. " 'Other orphans adopted by American families will be coming at the same time. We must find some responsible person going to America who will care for them on the way. We will keep in touch with you and let you know when your daughter is arriving.' ''

Julian tossed Eric into the air and caught him as he came down.

"Boy!" he exclaimed, "you're going to have a little sister! Any day now." He turned to Edie, "I'd better make sure we have six hundred dollars for her fare," he said.

"And I'd better get some clothes ready for her," said Edie. "She probably won't have any except what she's wearing."

The news spread quickly that the Garths were going to have a new baby. At once, some of their friends looked through their children's outgrown clothes and took to Edie those that a little girl might wear—dresses and panties, shoes and socks, coats and sweaters—more than enough to dress Ginny for two or three years.

"When is she coming?" all of them asked.

"Any day now," Edie told them. "I expect," she added.

A week passed.

A month passed.

Another month passed. Still no further word about Ginny.

To introduce Ginny to her new family, Edie sent a picture of the three Garths to her in care of International Social Service. Another month passed—and another.

"Are there any rules to this game we're playing—this game called Waiting?" Julian wanted to know.

"Only that the players must have patience to win, I suppose," said Edie.

From the day Edie and Julian received the letter telling them about Ginny, ten long months passed. Finally, early one evening in November, the telephone rang, more insistently than usual, Edie thought as she picked up the receiver.

"I have a cablegram for Mr. and Mrs. Julian Garth," she heard a voice coming through the receiver.

"I am Mrs. Garth," answered Edie. "Julian!" she whispered excitedly. "I think this is it!"

" 'Your daughter arriving O'Hare Field Chicago December 1 Pacific Airlines,' " the voice read from the cablegram.

"She's coming," shouted Edie as she slammed down the receiver. "Julian, she's coming! Eric! Listen! Your little sister's coming!"

Joining hands, the three danced around the room.

Suddenly Edie announced, "We'd better come to our senses and get ready for Ginny. I'll phone Mother and Dad and ask if they can come and care for Eric while we go to Chicago to meet Ginny.''

Yes, Grandpa assured her, of course they could come. ''I've bought a little doll for you to take to her,'' he added. ''It's a cute little thing. I'll bring it along. And I'll bring some broccoli. I've heard that Chinese people like broccoli.''

Late on the afternoon of November 30, after Grandma and Grandpa had arrived, Edie and Julian drove to Chicago. At the airport they were told that Ginny's plane had run into strong head winds over the Pacific Ocean and would come in late. ''I'd advise you to get a night's sleep,'' the airlines agent told them. ''The plane is scheduled now to arrive about nine in the morning.''

''So our game of Waiting isn't over yet,'' said Julian as he and Edie made their way to a nearby motel.

Before eight the next morning they were back at the airport, hurrying to the gate where Ginny's plane was to arrive. This time there was little waiting. Almost at once, out of the murky morning dimness, the plane came in sight, a great bird blinking bright eyes as Julian and Edie watched it settle down on the runway and taxi toward the airport.

Off came passengers, streaming down the ramp and into the airport. Finally came a very small, very dainty Chinese woman leading two children. Behind her came a stewardess, carrying in her arms a tiny child.

Julian approached the Chinese lady.

''Are these the children for adoption?'' he asked.

''Yes. Yes, they are,'' answered the Chinese lady. ''They were sent in my care. Nine of them. Some went to Seattle, some to New York. These are all that are left.''

"How did you manage with so many?" asked Julian. "You must have been flying a long time."

"Thirty hours from Hong Kong." The Chinese lady laughed. "They kept me busy," she said, "feeding them and taking them to the toilet and washing them up."

"We are the Garths," said Julian. "We're looking for our daughter."

"The Garths? The stewardess has your daughter," the Chinese lady said.

As the stewardess laid Ginny in Edie's outstretched arms, the child howled her objection.

"Oh, not yet, maybe," said Edie, handing Ginny back to the stewardess.

In her hand, Edie noticed, Ginny tightly clutched a crumpled piece of paper. It was the picture of the Garths that Edie had sent her.

Together the group moved through the crowd to a quiet conference room in the airport. Other men and women joined them to claim their children.

Inside the room Edie handed Ginny the doll Grandpa Anderson had sent.

Ginny, still in the arms of the stewardess, drew back. She muttered some words in Chinese.

"She says for you to carry it," the Chinese lady translated the words.

Then the lady handed Julian the passport and visa that permitted Ginny to enter the United States. She gave him other papers, too, all of them belonging to Ginny and all important.

Finally, the time for parting came. Once more Edie took Ginny from the stewardess.

Ginny screamed in terror.

"We'd better get out of here," said Julian, "before people begin wondering what we're doing to her."

Through the airport and all the way to the motel, Ginny continued to scream, and nothing Edie could think to say or do comforted her.

Back at the motel, Edie peeled a banana and offered it to Ginny. Ginny snatched it from her, stopped screaming, and crammed chunks of it into her mouth. When she had finished the banana, Edie gave her milk to drink. Ginny gulped that down.

"While she's stuffing herself, I'll bring the car," said Julian.

"I'll sit in the back seat with her," said Edie. "Maybe she'll go to sleep. She must be terribly tired as well as afraid."

Stretched out on the back seat of the car and covered warmly with blankets, Ginny fell asleep almost as soon as the car started.

At the first red light, Julian stopped the car and glanced back at Ginny.

"She's a pretty baby, isn't she?" he said. "Oh, but she's a pretty baby."

"Julian!" exclaimed Edie. "How can you say she's pretty when she's so scrawny and thin? I've seen scrawny children, but never in my life have I seen any child so wasted away as this."

Julian defended himself. "I'm seeing into the future. I'm seeing her when she's eight, and twelve. And twenty. She'll be pretty then. You don't deny that, do you?"

Edie looked at Ginny for several minutes. "I agree with

you about the future,'' she said. ''When Ginny is eight, or twelve, or twenty, she'll be very pretty.''

As the car stopped in front of the Garth apartment, the door burst open. Out rushed Grandma and Grandpa Anderson and Eric.

''Want to see my sister,'' demanded Eric.

Edie pulled back the blankets from around Ginny's face and held the child low for Eric to see.

A slow grin spread over his face. He looked from Ginny to Edie. As the others watched, he put out a finger and touched Ginny's cheek. He looked back at Edie and smiled happily.

''Lunch is ready. Let me carry my new granddaughter in,'' said Grandma.

Edie laid Ginny in Grandma's arms.

''Why, this child is nothing but skin and bones,'' declared Grandma. ''Somebody has let her starve.''

''She's starved because there wasn't food enough to give her,'' explained Edie. ''And there are thousands more like her in Hong Kong who won't ever have a Grandma like you.''

In the living room, Eric danced around Ginny, showing her his toys and chattering to her. Ginny looked about her, frightened.

''She won't talk to me,'' complained Eric.

''She doesn't understand what you're saying, Eric,'' Edie explained. ''She talks and understands only Chinese words. But soon she'll understand you. We'll all help her learn the words we say.''

Grandpa sat looking at Ginny.

"I declare," he said, shaking his head, "that child looks like a bird. A scrawny, picked bird."

Edie noticed a tear running down Grandpa's cheek.

"All right, Grandpa," she said, "we'll eat lunch. We'll begin right now stuffing our little bird and putting some weight on her. I see Grandma has cooked some of the broccoli you brought."

Edie put Ginny in a high chair and set before her a plate of food. Immediately, with both hands, Ginny began cramming broccoli into her mouth.

"Here, let's eat with this," Edie said to Ginny, putting a spoon into her hand.

Ginny flung the spoon to the floor and continued to cram food into her mouth with both hands. She ate every tidbit on her plate and drained her cup of milk.

"Look at that!" said Grandpa. "Did you ever see the like of that?"

Edie refilled both plate and cup. Ginny cleaned the plate and drained the cup.

"You've had enough for now, Ginny dear," said Edie, moving the plate from Ginny's chair. "You might make yourself sick if you eat more now."

As Ginny saw her plate disappear, she screamed with rage.

"Well, just a little more," agreed Edie.

Edie placed before her a plate half filled with food. But Ginny could cram down no more. She stared at the food.

As Edie lifted the plate to remove it from the chair, Ginny grabbed it and screamed again.

"Listen, Ginny dear," said Edie, wiping a tear from her

own eyes. "I'll save it for you. You shall have it. It's nap-time now. When you wake up, I'll give it to you."

Grandma and Grandpa, Julian and Eric watched as Edie took off Ginny's clothes and put a nightie on her.

"Why did they let that baby starve like that?" Grandpa asked again. No one answered.

Edie put Ginny in her crib in the children's room. Eric climbed into his crib nearby and lay down.

Ginny refused to lie down. She stood clinging to the side of the crib and screaming. She screamed until her face turned blue.

"What do we do now?" Edie asked Julian.

"Maybe she's never slept in a bed," suggested Julian.

"In that case, I know only one thing to try," said Edie. "I'll spread a blanket on the floor here in the living room and see if she'll sleep on that."

Only when Edie herself lay on the blanket did Ginny lie down. She stopped screaming and sucked her thumb, but she didn't sleep. In a few minutes she was up, wandering about the room on her weak, wobbly legs. Soon she found one of Eric's toys he had left in the living room—a little red automobile. She was clutching it in her arms when Eric woke up from his nap and came into the room.

"No!" he scolded as he caught sight of Ginny with his toy. "No! No!" he scolded, over and over.

"Why don't you let her play with it?" asked Edie. "She's probably never had a toy. She won't hurt it."

"No!" said Eric. "She's got a doll. She can play with her doll."

"I see all of us have something to learn," said Edie,

half to herself. "Learning to share is as important as Ginny's learning to speak English."

Two months passed before Ginny consented to take a nap in her own bed. Usually the naps were short.

One afternoon when the nap was ended, Edie heard voices coming from the children's room—laughing, singing voices. Blended together, they sounded to Edie like a small miracle.

Softly, she opened the door to find Eric and Ginny each standing up in bed. They were singing the same song, "Jesus Loves Me," Eric in English, Ginny in Chinese, and jumping up and down as they sang.

Softly, Edie closed the door and tiptoed away.

3

And Angela

One September morning, ten months after Ginny joined the
Garth family, Julian yawned, stretched, opened his eyes,
and looked at the clock.

"Edie!" he exclaimed, throwing back the covers. "It's
morning!"

Edie, her eyes only half open, yawned. She glanced at
the clock.

"Seven o'clock! We haven't slept this late— Do you
know what that means?" she asked. "It means Ginny has
slept all night. Straight through the night. The first time
since she came."

"And we've slept too," said Julian. "Do you suppose,
since she has slept through one night, she isn't going to
wake up and cry at night anymore? And we won't have to
crawl out of bed and bring her milk because she's hungry?"

"We can at least begin to hope," said Edie. She got out of bed and hurried toward the kitchen. "I'd forgotten what it's like to sleep the whole night through."

"At last, our Ginny's growing up," said Julian, as he joined Edie in the kitchen. "Her legs and arms are filling out. She grows prettier every day, and—"

"And have you noticed how well she's beginning to speak in English?" asked Edie. "She says most words very plainly."

Julian laughed. "But not *Eric,*" he said. "Eric gets so mad when she calls him *Ek.*"

After the family had eaten their breakfast in the kitchen, Julian left for the university. While Edie cleared the breakfast table, Eric and Ginny disappeared into their room. Eric soon returned, lugging an armful of books. At his heels followed Ginny with a doll in her arms.

"Read, Mommie, read," begged Eric.

"Read about Peter Rabbit," said Ginny.

She and Eric hurried to the living room and stood beside the rocking chair in which Edie usually sat when she read to them. There they waited.

"Will one book this morning be enough?" called Edie from the kitchen.

Neither Eric nor Ginny replied. They waited until Edie had piled the breakfast dishes in the sink and had come to sit in the rocking chair. Then Ginny, clutching her doll, climbed on one knee while Eric with his armful of books climbed on the other.

Edie looked through the well-worn books until she found *The Tale of Peter Rabbit.* As she read the story, each page was turned by Ginny almost before it was finished.

"Now," suggested Edie, when she had read the last page, "why don't you two run and play while I wash the dishes?"

There was no answer. Instead, Eric went hastily through the books again while Ginny watched eagerly. He found *Katy and the Big Snow* and opened it for Edie. "Read!" he commanded.

When Edie had finished reading *Katy and the Big Snow,* she announced, "That's all for this morning. Eric, why don't you and Ginny look through your books now and find what you want me to read tomorrow?"

Eric gathered up his books and left the room. Ginny walked behind him, in his footsteps, dragging her doll by one arm.

In the evening after supper, while Julian studied in the big bedroom, the children put on their pajamas and hurried again to the rocking chair to wait for Edie. Again they climbed onto her knees.

"It's singing time," said Edie. "What shall it be first?"

" 'Mary Had a Little Lamb,' " chose Ginny.

"You and Eric sing with me," suggested Edie.

Together, the three sang "Mary Had a Little Lamb."

"What song do you want, Eric?" asked Edie when they had finished "Mary."

"Uh—uh—'Lavender's Blue,' " chose Eric.

Together the three sang "Lavender's Blue." Ginny stumbled through many of the words.

"What's dilly dilly?" she asked.

"A dilly might be one of several things," Edie explained. "The yellow flower we call a daffodil is sometimes called a dilly."

"A dilly dilly is two daffodils, Ginny," said Eric. "Sing more, Mommie."

"Just one more song," announced Edie. "What shall it be?"

" 'The Puffabellies'!" shouted Eric and Ginny together. "The Puffabellies" was always the last song of the evening. Together they sang:

> "Down at the station,
> Early in the morning,
> See the little puffabellies
> All in a row.
> See the engine driver
> Pull a little lever.
> Chug! Chug! Whoo! Whoo!
> Off we go!"

"Chug! Chug! Whoo! Whoo! Off we go!" called Julian from the bedroom. He hurried into the living room, picked the children up by their ankles, first Ginny and then Eric, carried them head downward, one at a time, and dropped them, giggling shrilly, into their beds.

Before Eric and Ginny were born, a fierce war had been fought in the faraway country of Korea. Thousands of American soldiers had been sent to Korea to fight in the war. Several years passed before the war was ended.

But the suffering caused by the war did not end. It went

on and on. In many places, the children suffered most of all. The fathers and mothers of thousands of them had been killed. Many mothers, if they were fortunate enough to be alive, had no way to earn money to buy food for their children, nor to keep them warm in winter. Often Edie and Julian talked about the Korean children and their suffering.

"Now that Ginny is feeling at home with us," said Edie to Julian one October evening after the children were in bed, "don't you think we ought to think about adopting another orphan?"

"You haven't forgotten our plan, have you?" asked Julian. "Two children of our own and two adopted Mexican-Americans? We could still adopt one Mexican-American," he said.

"Or," said Edie, "we could adopt two more children and not have any more of our own. Then we'd have our four, and our family would be finished. And," she added, "I've been thinking we ought to apply for a Korean orphan. A boy maybe? And afterward adopt a Mexican-American girl."

"Let's think this over awhile," suggested Julian.

After a week of thinking, and talking, and counting their money carefully, Edie and Julian went again to the local welfare agency. They would like themselves and their home to be approved for the adoption of another orphan, they told the social worker. Not just any orphan, they told her. An orphan from Korea. Oh, no, not just any orphan from Korea. They'd like to have a boy at least two years younger than Eric and Ginny. They'd especially like to have a little black boy from Korea.

The social worker was puzzled. She asked many questions. Why didn't they adopt an American child? They already had one Oriental child. There were so many American children waiting for adoption. "And why black?" she asked.

"Because there are many black orphans in Korea, left from the war there and from the American occupation of Korea after the war. Life for them is hard," Edie told her. "Even harder than for other orphans."

The social worker sighed and shook her head.

"You're determined?" she asked.

"Determined," said Julian.

"All you need do now is to approve us," said Edie. "Then we'll ask International Social Service to find us the kind of boy we want."

"Well," said Julian to Edie, as they left the social worker's office and started home, "do you feel as if you're about to be a mother again?"

"And you?" asked Edie. "Do you feel as if you're about to be a father again? I wonder—I just wonder," she continued, "what this son will be like."

"I've thought of a name for him," announced Julian.

"A name will make him more real to us," said Edie. "What is it?"

"Mark," said Julian. "Do you like that?"

"Yes. Yes, I think I do," agreed Edie. "Tonight we'll write to the people at International Social Service and ask them to get busy finding Mark. We don't want to have to wait for him as long as we waited for Ginny."

"Shall we tell Eric and Ginny right away?" asked

Julian. "Let them share the excitement from the beginning?"

"Of course," agreed Edie.

"Tell them tonight," suggested Julian. "At bedtime. It
will make a marvelous bedtime story."

When Edie and Julian reached home, they found that the
postman had been there. In the mailbox was an envelope
addressed to both of them. It came from a welfare agency in
Indiana.

"Wonder why an Indiana agency is writing to us," said
Julian as he tore open the envelope. Together he and Edie
read the letter.

" 'We understand that you like children,' " it began.
" 'We have a lovely little girl, part black, part white, part
American Indian, almost one month old, born September 6.
We want to put her up for adoption. We wonder if you
would be interested in her?"

Julian and Edie looked at each other. They laughed.

"People say opportunity never knocks twice," said
Julian. "But it surely knocks more than once if word gets
around that you want to adopt a child. What shall we do
with this letter?" he asked. "Forget it?"

"Let's forget it till after supper, anyway," said Edie.
"But let's tell the children about Mark."

When Ginny and Eric had been whoo-whooed to bed by
Julian, Edie followed them into the bedroom.

"Children," she said, "your father and I have something important to tell you."

"A bedtime story?" asked Ginny.

"What's it about?" Eric wanted to know.

"It is a bedtime story," said Edie, "and it's about a little boy."

"About me?" asked Eric.

"No, about another little boy," Edie told him. "You and Ginny are going to have a little brother."

"Where's he coming from?"

"When's he coming?"

"Where's he going to sleep?"

"What's his name?"

Questions came flooding from Ginny and Eric.

"We don't know just when he's coming," Julian told them. "We hope it won't be long. Three or four months, maybe. Maybe longer."

"He's coming on an airplane," added Edie.

"I came on an airplane," said Ginny, her eyes brightening. "Didn't I come on an airplane, Mommie?"

"And your little brother will come on an airplane, too. From a faraway country called Korea," said Edie.

"His name is Mark," Julian told them.

"Now you can go to sleep thinking about Mark," said Edie. "Good night."

As Edie and Julian left the room, they heard Eric whispering to himself: "Mark. Mark. Mark."

Later in the evening, Edie asked Julian, "Have you thought any more about the Indiana orphan? We'll have to write something to the agency—yes, or no."

Julian did not answer right away. Finally, "It would be nice, wouldn't it," he said, "having a little baby again? Remember how it was when Eric was a little baby?"

"How could I forget?" asked Edie. "But do you think

we can manage with two new children at once? Whatever
we decide about the Indiana baby, I feel we must have
Mark.''

"I agree with you,'' said Julian.

That evening Edie wrote a letter to International Social
Service, asking for a Korean orphan for the Garths—a boy,
black, two years younger than Ginny and Eric.

Three evenings later, Julian said, "If we hadn't already
applied for the Korean child—''

"It will be months, maybe years, I'm thinking, before
the Korean child joins the Garth family,'' said Edie.

"Had you realized,'' asked Julian, "that baby girl in Indiana is just the right age to fit into our family? She's more
than three years younger than Eric and Ginny. And she'll be
younger than Mark. At least a year younger.''

"And had you realized,'' asked Edie, "that if we adopt
her, she'll be Number Four. There will be our family—two
boys, two girls. Are we giving up altogether our idea of
another baby of our own?''

"With so many orphans and neglected children in the
world wanting a home and loving care,'' said Julian, "I
wonder if—if we shouldn't give up the idea? Just forget all
about another baby of our own?''

After several minutes of thought Edie answered. "I
think I'm willing,'' she said. "You said long ago there were
too many children in the world. So we won't add to the
number.''

"What should we do to get the Indiana baby? Should we
go to see her?'' asked Julian.

"We have to ask the agency here to write to the agency
in Indiana about us and our family,'' said Edie. "Then the

Indiana agency will give us more information about the baby. If we apply for her now, I think we may have her by Christmas.''

"A new baby for Christmas!" exclaimed Julian. "Let's go to the agency tomorrow."

The next day, Edie and Julian appeared at the home agency with the letter from the Indiana agency. The social worker read it and smiled.

"I'm glad you've given up the idea of adopting the Korean child," she said.

"Oh," said Edie, "we haven't given up that idea at all."

"This is another child," explained Julian. "This, with the Korean boy, will make four children for us. We intended all along to have four children. That completes the Garth family."

The social worker looked at Julian and sighed. She asked many questions: How did Eric and Ginny get along together? How big was the apartment in which the Garths lived?

"That's big enough for three children," she said when Julian told her the size of the apartment. "But suppose the Korean boy arrives soon? What will you do then?"

"Just what we did when Ginny came," Julian told her. "Find an apartment with more room."

"What is your salary, Mr. Garth?" the social worker asked.

Julian told her.

The social worker shook her head. "You can never support a family of six on that salary," she told him.

"It won't be long," Julian told her, "before I finish my

studying and teaching at the university here. Then I expect
to teach at a larger salary.''

"In that case," said the social worker, sighing again, "I
guess there's nothing we can do but approve you.''

"Soon?" asked Edie. "We'd like to have the baby by
Christmas.''

"As soon as possible," promised the social worker.
"This week, at least.''

"Should we tell Eric and Ginny now?" asked Julian
when he and Edie were on the street again and hurrying
home.

"I think not tonight," advised Edie. "Think how disappointed they'd be if we promised them a baby sister for
Christmas and something went wrong with our plans.''

Several letters traveled between the Indiana agency and
the Garths. Since the baby would have to be taken across a
state line, considerable time was needed to file the necessary papers, the agency in Indiana reported.

"Be patient," advised one letter that arrived on a chilly
November day. "We're sure you will have your baby by
Christmas.''

When Eric and Ginny were in their beds that evening,
Edie said to them, "Daddy and I have something to tell
you.''

"A story?" asked Eric.

"Yes," said Edie. "A story about a little baby. It's a
Christmas story.''

"About the baby Jesus?" asked Eric.

"No," said Julian. "This is a story about another baby.
A little girl baby.''

"What's the name of the baby?" asked Eric.

Edie and Julian looked at each other.

"She hasn't any name yet," Julian explained to the children. "Why don't we give her a name now?"

"Ginny," suggested Ginny.

"There's only one Ginny," Edie told her. "There could never be another like you. So we should give her some other name."

"I thought she was going to be a brother," said Eric.

"Not this one," explained Julian. "The brother is coming later."

"What would you like to name your baby sister?" asked Edie. She recited names: Mary. Ruth. Hannah. Gloria. Angela.

"Angela!" said Julian. "Angela's just right for a Christmas baby. Does everybody agree?"

"Will she get presents for Christmas?" asked Eric.

"Of course," said Edie. "Maybe you'd like to give her one of your books."

Eric shook his head. "She can't have my books," he said. "I'll give her—I'll give her—maybe I'll give her—"

"Why don't you think a few days before you decide what to give her?" suggested Julian. "And you, too, Ginny. You can go to sleep thinking about it. Good night, now."

One December day Edie found in the Garth mailbox a letter from the Indiana agency. It read: "Come for your baby on December 21."

On December 20, Julian and Edie bundled up Eric and

Ginny against the frosty cold and set out in their car for
Grandpa and Grandma Andersons' house in Indiana.

"Will Grandpa have bocci?" Ginny wanted to know.

"Grandpa's probably getting the broccoli out of the
freezer this minute, and soon he'll be looking out the window to see if you're coming," Edie told her.

The next morning Julian and Edie left Eric and Ginny
for Grandma and Grandpa Anderson to care for. "Grandma
will care for them and Grandpa will spoil them," said Edie.
Then they set out for the city where the baby to be named
Angela was waiting. On their arrival at the agency, they
were warmly welcomed by the superintendent while a nurse
was sent for Angela. Returning with a small bundle in her
arms, the nurse turned back the blankets to show Edie and
Julian the cuddly little tan-skinned baby inside.

"Why—she's perfect!" exclaimed Edie.

"She's beautiful!" beamed Julian as he leaned over the
baby. "Hello, Angela!" he said. "Welcome to the Garth
family!"

Angela smiled up at him, a big, toothless smile.

"That smile would capture anybody," declared Julian.

"I can see it has captured you," Edie told him, teasingly. "Completely. Heart and soul."

While the social worker gave Julian the papers necessary for the adoption of Angela, Edie laid the baby in a
basket she had brought and covered her warmly with blankets. Julian carried the basket to the car, and away they
drove to the Andersons' house. On the way, snow began to
fall—thick, heavy, wet snow.

"This makes it perfect!" declared Julian. "Snow, and a

little new baby, and hurrying home to Grandma and
Grandpa's house at Christmastime. Wonder what Eric and
Ginny are doing now?''

"Watching out the window," said Edie, "waiting for
Angela."

When Edie, Julian, and Angela reached the Andersons'
at dusk, the front door of the house was flung open and out
rushed Eric and Ginny, followed by Grandma and Grandpa
Anderson, Aunt Mary, Aunt Betsy, and Cousin John.

"Hurry in out of the cold!" urged Grandma Anderson
as Julian carried the basket up the walk. The others crowded
behind him.

In the big old-fashioned living room, a cheery wood fire
burned in the fireplace. It shone on the Christmas tree and
set all the tinsel to shimmering.

"Turn on the lights!" shouted Eric. "Turn on the lights
for Angela to see!"

He ran to turn on the lights of the Christmas tree. Ginny
edged close to the basket, elbowing her way among the
grownups.

"Grandma," asked Julian, "wouldn't you like to be the
first to hold your new granddaughter?"

Grandma lifted Angela out of the basket. Holding the
baby, she sat beside the fire and rocked her in her arms.
Ginny, standing beside her, slipped a finger inside Angela's
tiny hand. "She squeeze!" she said, screwing up her face
in delight.

Eric left the Christmas tree and hurried to stand beside
Ginny.

"Look at her! Look at Angela! She's laughing!"

"This is perfect, isn't it?" said Aunt Betsy. "A baby at Christmastime?"

Grandpa hummed the first line of a carol. The others, Ginny and Eric, too, joined in:

"The little Lord Jesus laid down His sweet head.
The stars in the sky looked down where He lay,
The little Lord Jesus, asleep on the hay."

Aunt Mary got up from her chair and, standing beside Grandpa, looked down at Angela. "This, it seems to me," she said thoughtfully, "is what Christmas is all about."

4

And Gene

Like Eric and Ginny, Angela ate and slept and grew. She slept more than Ginny but less than Eric at the time they joined the Garth family. Often she cried at night until Julian or Edie crawled sleepily out of bed, warmed milk for her, and brought it in a bottle. But every morning she awoke with a smile for anyone who came near.

While Edie put breakfast on the kitchen table, Julian fed Angela her morning milk, with Ginny and Eric hanging over his knees and begging to help hold the bottle. Now and then Angela let go of the nipple and smiled at them. When she had finished her milk, the three of them burped her. Then Ginny and Eric ran for Angela's clothes and Julian dressed her.

"Feeding Angela, with her cooing and smiling," said Julian one morning at breakfast, "puts me in a good mood for the whole day. Even if I've had to get up in the night to bring her milk,'' he added.

"Yes, I know," said Edie, teasingly. "Angela could ask for the moon and all the stars, and you would try to get them for her."

As she usually did each morning and afternoon, Edie fed Angela cereal and vegetable and fruit in the kitchen. Then she carried her to the rocking chair in the living room to give her milk. No sooner had Edie sat down in the chair with Angela in her arms and the bottle of milk in one hand than Eric, clutching an armful of books, climbed onto one knee.

"Read, Mommie, read," he ordered.

Ginny climbed onto Edie's other knee. "Read about Ping," she ordered.

Edie gathered all of the children into her arms.

"I can hold three of you at once," she told them. "But my lap isn't big enough to hold four. What are we going to do when Mark comes?"

"Let him sit on the floor," said Eric.

"Read, Mommie," demanded Ginny.

Edie read to them *Ping* and *Pet Parade*.

"Now," she said, "while I put Angela to bed for her nap, you two can play here quietly in the living room."

One Saturday morning when Julian was home, a letter arrived from International Social Service in New York. Edie tore open the envelope quickly.

" 'We think we have just the boy you are looking for,' " she read to Julian. " 'He was born on April 18, 1960.' "

"Exactly the right age," said Julian. "Almost two

years younger than Eric and Ginny. And about a year and a half older than Angela. What else?''

" 'His mother was a Korean woman,' " read Edie, " 'his father a black American soldier.' "

"Just what we asked for," commented Julian. "Anything more?"

" 'The mother kept the child for a year after he was born,' " read Edie. " 'Then, because she was unable to care for him, and to provide him with food and shelter—' "

"Poor kid!" said Julian. "His mother was probably having to live in the streets and scrounge for food."

" '—she took the child to the World Vision Orphanage in the city of Seoul in Korea,' " read Edie. "That's all."

"Probably the most loving thing she could do was to give the boy up and put him in an orphanage," said Julian. "I've always thought the most loving thing Ginny's mother could have done was to leave her where she knew somebody would find her and care for her."

"Two years in an orphanage in a country torn apart by war! I doubt if Mark has had enough to eat," said Edie. "With so many homeless children, I feel sure there was never food enough to go around. And imagine how frightened and lonely many of these children must have been. And I doubt if there was ever love enough to go around."

"Do you think we have enough love for Mark, after we've given Eric and Ginny and Angela all that's due them?" asked Julian.

"The more one loves, the more love grows," Edie reminded him. "Let's get Mark here just as soon as possible. Angela's been so easy to care for that I think a fourth child will be no trouble at all."

The next day Edie wrote a letter to the people at International Social Service. Yes, she told them, the Garths very much wanted the Korean boy. They felt that he was exactly the boy to fit into their family.

"Now I hope we don't have to play that waiting game we played with Ginny so long," said Edie as she sealed the envelope.

"Remember what you told me," Julian reminded her. "Waiting will teach us patience. And," he added, "we may need some patience."

Edie and Julian waited. And they waited.

All through the year and into the next summer they waited.

While they waited, things happened that were of great importance to the Garth family.

First, Julian finished his work at the university and was awarded a doctor of philosophy degree.

"This is yours as much as mine," he said to Edie as he handed her his diploma.

Second, in August, Julian received a letter from a university in Indiana. Would he come there to teach in the fall, the letter asked.

There was great excitement in the Garth household when Julian and Edie read the letter. Julian accepted the offer. For two days, he and Edie talked about little else.

"It means moving to a new city where we know no one, and no one knows us. You realize that," said Julian to Edie.

"But we've moved before to a city where no one knew us, and we've made friends," Edie reminded him. "It will be even easier to make friends now," she added. "We have the children. They'll help us."

"Do you suppose we may buy a house there, and bring up the children in their own home?" Julian asked.

"If we can find one we can afford," said Edie. "It would be wonderful to have a house with a yard where the children can play and bring their friends to play with them."

"Poor kids!" said Julian. "Living always in an apartment as they've been doing they don't even know what it's like to run barefoot on grass."

"And trees," said Edie. "We must find a yard with trees they can climb and where they can have a swing and can picnic in the shade."

"Are you remembering that Eric and Ginny will be old enough to start kindergarten this fall?" asked Julian.

"Maybe Ginny had better wait awhile," said Edie. "It won't hurt her to have another year for growing before she starts kindergarten. Wonder what kind of schools the city has."

"Why don't you and I drive over to the university?" suggested Julian. "We can talk to the people there, find out more about my job, and ask about the schools. And," he added, "we can look for a house."

"Good idea!" declared Edie. "But we'll have to work fast. Summer is almost gone. In less than a month you'll begin teaching."

Two days later, while a friend cared for the children, Edie and Julian spent an exciting day in the Indiana city. They had much to tell the children when they returned home. Julian had learned more about his classes at the university; they had found an excellent school where Eric would attend kindergarten; and, best of all, they had bought a house—a big, old-fashioned, rambling house with plenty of room for themselves and four children, and a big yard for running and playing.

"And mowing the grass," put in Julian.

"Can I take my dolls?" asked Ginny.

"Of course," said Edie.

"If Ginny takes all her dolls, can I take all my books?" asked Eric.

"Of course," said Julian. "There's room for every-thing."

"What will Angela take?" asked Ginny.

"I'll give you and Eric three boxes, Ginny," said Edie. "I'll mark one for you, one for Eric, and one for Angela. Each of you may put into your box whatever you want to take to your new home. You and Eric together may pack Angela's box for her."

Ginny went to work at once. She ransacked the apart-ment for toys and threw them helter-skelter into the boxes.

"Don't you touch my books!" Eric ordered her. "You don't pack right."

Edie, too, began to pack.

"All the baby clothes are outgrown by this time," she said to Julian, "and we won't have any further use for them. I'll give them to some mother who needs them. And I suppose there's no use taking baby toys with us either," she added. "I'll give them all away with the clothes."

Through the apartment she hurried, collecting outgrown baby clothes and baby shoes and socks, collecting, too, balls and rattles and toys that make a racket when pulled.

Into a box they went to be given to a friend who had a small baby.

On still another box Edie printed in big, bold letters, MARK.

"If he's like Ginny when she came, he won't be nearly as big as he ought to be," she said.

Into the box went Eric's largest outgrown clothes. Into the box, too, went some of Eric's outgrown toys—a fire engine, a small bat, some tiny trucks and railroad cars.

Then, early one morning, two weeks before the Garths were to move to Indiana, a third thing of great importance happened.

The telephone rang. Edie hurried to answer it.

"Mrs. Garth?" came a voice through the receiver.

Edie recognized the voice. It belonged to the superintendent of the orphanage in Indiana from which they had brought Angela.

"I have a wonderful little boy saved for you," said the superintendent.

"What?" Edie's voice exploded.

"I have a wonderful little boy that would just fit into your home," continued the superintendent. "He's a lovely child. His parentage is mixed. So far as we've been able to learn, he's part American Indian, part black, and part white. And because you and your husband—bless you!—specialize in cases such as this, I thought of you."

"Well—" Edie hesitated. "How old is the boy?" she asked.

"Nearly seven months," said the superintendent.

Again Edie hesitated.

"I don't really know how—you see, we're expecting another child almost any day now. From Korea. I—I don't know what we'd do with five children. We've always planned to have only four. And with two new ones at once—well—I really don't know how we'd manage. Of course the Korean child we're going to have is now three and a half, but he won't be able to understand English, and that will be an added difficulty."

"Do you want to think it over?" asked the superintendent.

"Of course," said Edie, "we had Ginny and Angela at almost the same time and we've got along fine with them. Angela's hardly more than a baby. Still, we might be able to manage. But," she added, "we're moving in two weeks. To Indiana. Julian will be teaching there. We've bought a house there, too, and it will take us some time to get squared around. Of course, the house is big enough for a fifth child."

"If you're moving to Indiana, you wouldn't have to go through the red tape and the waiting to take the child across a state line," the superintendent told her. "You could take him right away."

"Well—" Edie paused. "Julian and I will talk this over thoroughly, and in a few days I'll phone you. Is that all right?"

"Fine!" said the superintendent. "I'll be waiting to hear."

In the evening when songs had been sung, and Julian had picked each of the children up by the ankles and carried them, screaming and laughing, to bed, he and Edie sat down in the kitchen to talk.

"Five mouths to feed," said Julian when Edie had reported to him her conversation with the superintendent. "Five heads to educate. Five sets of teeth to straighten. Five—"

"Five children to get off to school every morning," added Edie. "Five sets of clothes to launder. Arguments to settle. Cuts to bandage. Mumps. Sore throats."

Suddenly they both laughed.

"We sound as if we're sorry for ourselves," said Julian.

"When, in fact, we ought to consider ourselves privileged," said Edie. "But what shall we do about this fifth child?"

"Let's call him Eugene, shall we?" suggested Julian. "Gene."

"Then we're taking him?" asked Edie.

"Let's tell the superintendent we'll drive down and have a look at him," suggested Julian.

"And I've just given away all the baby clothes," Edie reminded him.

"I expect we'll find mothers in our new home town who have outgrown children's clothes they'll be glad to give away," said Julian.

Early the next day Edie telephoned the superintendent.

"We've decided we'll come down in a couple of weeks and look at the child," Edie told her. "We're not promising to take him. But we'll look at him."

In two weeks the Garths moved to their new home in Indiana. In two days they settled in. Then they put Eric, Ginny, and Angela into their car and drove to Grandma and Grandpa Andersons'. On the way Edie and Julian told the children about Gene.

"Goody!" exclaimed Ginny and clapped her hands.

"I'll give him some of my toys," said Eric. "But he'll have to stay out of my books."

"He isn't ready for books yet," Edie told Eric. "Anyway, we aren't sure we're going to bring him home with us. We're just going to see him."

"Aw, Mommie!" Disappointed voices rose from the back seat.

The next morning Edie and Julian started for the orphanage, leaving Eric, Ginny, and Angela with Grandma and Grandpa.

"Children," Grandma told them, "I feel in my bones you're about to have a new brother. Your father and mother say they're going to be hard-hearted about this one. 'Realistic.' That's what they call it. But you wait and see."

At the orphanage the superintendent greeted them warmly.

"I must tell you one thing more about this child," she said. "He has recently had an operation for hernia. After the operation we placed him in a foster home, but, unfortunately, the foster mother decided it was easier to do things for him than to let him do things for himself. Or maybe she was afraid he'd hurt himself. So she has done everything for him. Now he has the idea he can't do anything for himself. He can't even roll over though there's no reason why he shouldn't. He thinks somebody has to turn him over."

"May we see him?" asked Edie.

"Sure. We'd like to take a look at the boy," said Julian.

A nurse brought the baby. He lay in a basket, whimpering.

Edie leaned over and spoke to him.

He began to wail.

"I believe this boy needs us," Julian said to Edie.

"He needs somebody," Edie said above the wailing. "Badly. Do you think we can cope with that?"

"Our other children have cried. Remember?" said Julian. "And we've coped. It seems—it's a pretty small problem, don't you think? Just letting the kid learn he can do a few things for himself?"

Edie turned to the superintendent.

"He looks like a fine, healthy boy," she said.

"All he needs to help him grow into a fine man is the love and the sensible care he'd have in your home," said the superintendent.

As Julian bent over the basket, the baby wailed louder.

"Evidently he does need us," said Edie. She turned to the superintendent. "I believe you said we might take him now?" she asked.

"Right now," said the superintendent. "I'll ask a nurse to get him ready while I get his papers in order. The adoption, of course, will come later."

In a short time, baby and papers were ready. The superintendent gave Edie a pillow for the baby to ride on and a jump seat for him to play in at home. And away drove Edie, Julian, and Gene toward the Andersons' house.

Gene didn't like the pillow for a bed. He screamed until Edie took him up and held him in her arms. There he fell asleep.

"Maybe we'd better hope he sleeps a lot!" said Julian, glancing at the child.

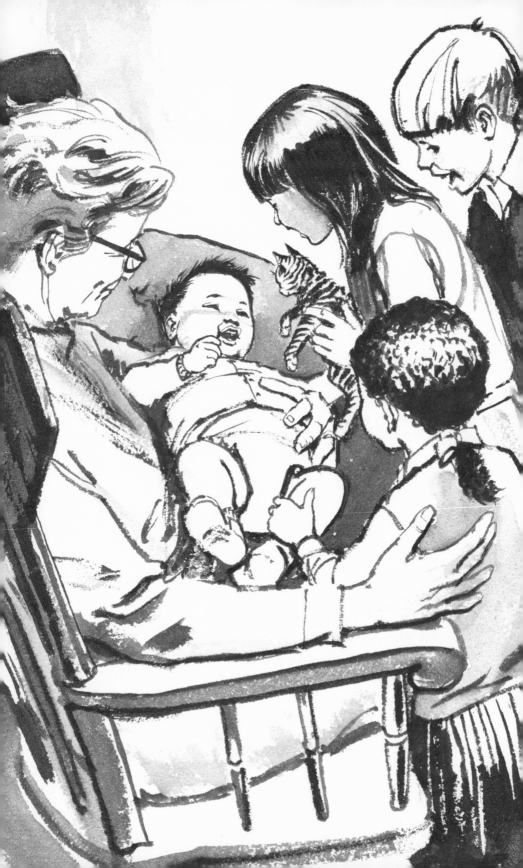

Dusk was overtaking them by the time they reached the Andersons' house.

Grandma Anderson hurried down the walk, with Eric, Ginny, and Angela at her heels. Angela was sucking milk from a bottle.

"We brought you a new grandson, Mother," said Edie quietly as she got out of the car with the sleeping baby in her arms. "His name is Gene."

"I expected him," said Grandma, laughing. "Didn't I say so, children?"

Gene stirred and opened his eyes.

"Come here, Gene, and let's get acquainted," said Grandma.

She took the baby tenderly from Edie's arms and started toward the house. Gene looked up at her and whimpered.

"There! There!" soothed Grandma as she carried him into the house and sat down in the rocking chair. The whimper grew to a howl.

The children, in awe, gathered around Grandma.

"What's the matter, baby?" cooed Ginny, trying to comfort him.

"Doesn't he like us?" asked Eric anxiously.

Angela stood watching Gene. She took the nipple of the bottle of milk from her mouth. Slowly she walked over to Gene and pushed the nipple into his mouth.

Gene stopped crying and for a minute sucked on the nipple. Then, with the nipple still in his mouth, he smiled at Angela.

"He laugh!" shouted Ginny, clapping her hands. "Gene laugh!" Everybody clapped—everybody but Gene. Frightened by the clapping, he burst out crying.

Grandpa Anderson left the room. Soon he returned, cuddling in his arms a small tiger-striped kitten.

"Tigger!" shouted Eric. "Just like Christopher Robin's Tigger!"

For a moment Eric, Ginny, and Angela forgot their new brother and rushed to stroke the kitten.

"Can we take him home with us, Grandpa?" Eric asked.

"I'll feed him. I'll feed him good," promised Ginny.

"Yes, you may take him home with you," said Grandpa. "He's for all of you."

He laid the kitten in Ginny's outstretched arms.

Ginny, holding the purring kitten close against her cheek, walked back to Gene.

"Look, Gene, what Grandpa gave us," she said, holding the kitten low enough for the baby to see. "You stop crying now and you hear him. He talking to you. He saying, 'Stop crying, Gene. Nobody going to hurt you. Everybody at Grandma's house like you.' "

Hearing Ginny's voice, Gene stopped crying. Hearing the purring of the kitten, he listened. Slowly, a smile broke over his face.

"Good!" Ginny exclaimed. "Good! You doing fine, Gene!"

5

And Mark

In early September, Eric started kindergarten. Leaving home every school day, alone, with a book in his hands, made him feel important. It made him feel a little frightened, too.

Ginny, too, felt important. With Eric out of the house, she was the oldest of the Garth children at home. At once she appointed herself the caretaker of the younger children, especially of Gene.

Each day Gene cried, but each day he cried less and smiled more than the day before. Ginny saw to that.

When Gene, on a blanket on the floor, tired of lying on his back and began to cry, Ginny brought Tigger and sat on the floor beside Gene with the kitten in her lap. She stroked Tigger's back, Tigger purred, and Gene stopped crying to look and listen.

"If you turn over on your side you can see Tigger better," Ginny told Gene.

Gene wanted to see Tigger better. He wanted to touch the kitten. He held up his hands.

"You can't reach Tigger that way," Ginny told him. "Why don't you turn over on your side? Then you can reach Tigger."

Gene whimpered.

"Isn't that too bad now!" said Ginny. "If you'd just turn over, you could see Tigger good. I'd let you pat him."

Gene wailed.

Ginny lifted Tigger out of her lap and for a few seconds held him high for Gene to see. Then she put the kitten back in her lap.

Gene continued to wail.

"Isn't it too bad, Tigger, that a big boy like Gene won't turn over?" said Ginny to the kitten.

As Gene wailed, he squirmed and kicked. Suddenly he flipped from his back to his right side. In his surprise, he stopped wailing.

"Good for you, Gene!" praised Ginny. "Mommie!" she shouted. "Come and see!"

When Edie came hurrying into the living room, she saw Gene on his right side with one hand on the back of the kitten that Ginny held close to him.

"Now, Gene," said Ginny, "guess what I'm going to do next. I'm going to sit on the other side of you and let you turn over again. All the way over to the other side. See?"

As Edie watched, Ginny, with Tigger in her arms, hurried to the other side of Gene and sat beside the blanket on which he lay.

"Now," she said, "if you turn this way you can put your hand on Tigger again."

Gene wailed and kicked, and then, all of a sudden, he squirmed and rolled himself over to his left side.

"Good boy!" Ginny praised Gene as she held Tigger near enough for him to touch. "Know what I'm going to do next, Mommie? I'm going to teach Gene to sit up."

"Whatever would I do without you, Ginny?" asked Edie as she hurried away to the kitchen.

At lunch Edie said to Julian, "We don't especially need another child in the house just now, but it's been weeks and weeks since we've heard anything from the people at International Social Service. Do you suppose we ought to write and ask if they have any idea when Mark will be here?"

"Why don't I telephone right now?" suggested Julian.

He dialed International Social Service in New York.

"Half an hour ago we got off a letter to you," said the man who answered Julian's call. "Special delivery. We heard within the last hour that your boy will arrive in Chicago on Sunday. Will you be there to meet him?"

"Let's see," said Julian. "Today is Thursday. Just two more days. All right," he assured the man. "We'll be at the airport."

"Who's coming, Daddy?" asked the children as Julian hung up the receiver.

"Mark's coming!" Julian announced. "On Sunday. Your mother and I will drive to Chicago to meet him at the airport."

"Whoopee!" shouted Eric.

"Would you like to go to Chicago with us, Eric, and meet him?" asked Edie.

"Will I see some big airplanes?" asked Eric.

"You'll see planes coming in or going out just about every minute," promised Julian.

"Whoopee!" shouted Eric again. Then, soberly, he asked, "Will Ginny and Angela and Gene stay at Grandma's?"

"Yes," said Edie. "We'll all drive down there on Saturday. Then you and your father and I will drive to Chicago to meet Mark on Sunday."

For a few seconds Eric was silent. Then, "I want to stay at Grandma's," he said.

"Why?" asked Julian. "You won't see any big airplanes at Grandma's."

"Don't you want to see your new brother?" asked Edie. "In the Garth family now, you will be Big Brother, Mark will be Middle-sized Brother, and Gene will be Little Brother. I think Mark would like to see his Big Brother when he gets off the plane."

"I want to stay at Grandma's," Eric repeated stubbornly.

"But think, Eric," said Julian. "Everything will be new and strange to Mark. He has never seen either your mother or me. Of course, he hasn't seen his Big Brother either. But I think he'd feel better if he saw a boy his size when he gets off the plane. We'll run down to the dime store and you can pick out something to give him. A new, shiny fire engine, maybe. Don't you suppose he'd like a fire engine?"

"I want to stay at Grandma's," Eric repeated.

"Why?" asked Edie.

"I want to see the cows," said Eric. "And Tigger wants to see the cows, too."

"Oh, that's it," said Julian. "Did Grandpa let you milk a cow the last time you were there?"

Eric nodded. "And he squirted some milk in my mouth. And then he squirted milk into the kittens' pan, and I watched the kittens drink it."

"Another time, Eric," Julian told him, "you can stay with Grandma and Grandpa and help Grandpa milk the cows. But this time we'd like you to go to Chicago with us to meet Mark."

"And now," said Edie, "we'd all better go into high gear and get ready for Mark. Ginny, you'll look after Gene, won't you? And Eric, why don't you hunt up some of your toys to share with Mark when he gets here?"

"Not my books," said Eric. "He can't have my books."

"He couldn't read your books now, Eric," explained Edie. "He won't even be able to talk with you because he doesn't know English."

"Can't he talk to anybody?" asked Eric.

"Not at first," Edie told him. "We'll have to be very patient with him and help him learn English."

"I'll help him," offered Ginny. "I learned English."

"We'll all help him," said Julian.

While Julian and Eric went looking for a fire engine, Edie hustled about the house, getting a bed in Eric's room ready for Mark, thinking of food he might like to eat, of ways to help him understand what the Garths would be saying to him.

On Saturday, the Garths drove to Grandma and Grandpa Andersons' house, taking Tigger with them. On Sunday morning early, so early that the sun had not yet come up and a few stars could still be seen blinking palely in the sky, Edie, Julian, and Eric set out for O'Hare International Airport in Chicago.

"What will Gene look like?" asked Eric as they drove along the highway.

"I think he'll look different from all the rest of us," Edie told him. "He'll be darker, I'm sure. I wonder if we'll recognize him. There will likely be other children with him."

Julian, Edie, and Eric reached the airport an hour ahead of the time Mark's plane was scheduled to arrive. They found a window where they could watch planes land and take off. There they waited.

With his nose pressed against the window, Eric watched fascinated as blue planes and white planes and silver planes, planes with golden tails, planes with red, white, and blue stripes on their noses, and planes bearing big green circles landed and took off in a steady stream.

"I don't believe he's missing the cows a great deal," said Julian to Edie, smiling as Eric excitedly pointed out to them one plane after another.

Suddenly, over the loud speaker, came the announcement the Garths had been listening for: "Pacific Airlines Plane, Flight Number 360, arriving at Gate 40."

"That's it, Eric! That's Mark's plane! Hear?" called Julian.

He took Eric by the hand. "Let's go!" he said.

Leading Eric through a crowd of people, Edie and Julian arrived at Gate 40 in time to see a great plane hover over the field, alight on the runway with a bounce, taxi along for a distance, and come to a stop at the unloading ramp. Passengers streamed off—men and women, families with little boys and little girls, tall people and short people, plump and slender, old and young—all of them hurrying away somewhere. Finally the Garths, craning their necks, caught sight of two small black boys coming off together, holding hands and looking a little frightened. A tall man followed close behind.

"There they are!" said Julian. "See?"

He lifted Eric to his shoulder. Edie stood on tiptoe to see.

When the tall man and the boys reached the Garths, Julian held out his hand.

"My name is Julian Garth and this is my wife, Edie," he said. "I believe one of these boys is our son."

"How do you do?" said the man, shaking hands with both of them. "This boy is yours," he said, laying his hand on the shoulder of the darker boy. "He's quite a boy," he added.

Inside a conference room the man and the Garths talked briefly. The man gave them Mark's passport, his visa, and other important papers that Mark needed. He shook hands with Julian and Edie, and then with Eric. "Take good care of your new brother now," he said to Eric. Last of all, he shook hands with Mark and said something to him in Korean that the Garths couldn't understand. Then, taking the other boy by the hand, he led him away.

When the Garths came out of the conference room, they found the crowd had thinned. Edie took Mark's right hand. Eric held out to him the little shiny fire engine.

Mark took the engine, but he didn't look at it. He didn't look at Eric. He seemed not to look at anyone or anything as he was led by Edie toward the exit.

At the exit, he began making whimpering noises.

"I think you'd better carry him, Julian," Edie said.

Julian picked up Mark, held him close to his shoulder, and spoke soothing words to him.

"What's the matter with Mark?" asked Eric. "Can't he walk?"

"He's afraid because everything is strange to him," explained Edie. "New and strange."

"They aren't new and strange to me," said Eric.

"But you must remember that Mark has never seen us before," said Edie. "He doesn't know who we are nor where we are taking him. And he isn't used to airports and mobs of people rushing in every direction. Most of his life he has lived in an orphanage filled with children like himself. Besides, he must be tired after flying thousands of miles. And, since he doesn't understand English, he doesn't know what we're saying to him."

"Then why do we talk to him?" asked Eric.

"Even though he can't understand what we say," Edie explained, "he can understand the way we say it. If we speak kindly to him, he knows we love him. He will soon learn not to be afraid of us."

They found their car in the parking lot. "I'm going to let you two boys sit on the back seat," said Edie, "and maybe

Mark will play with the fire engine. But before we start, I want to see if he'd like something to eat. He's probably hungry.''

Edie peeled a banana, broke it in two, and held one piece out to Mark; the other she gave to Eric. Mark looked at his piece for a moment, shrank back into his corner of the seat, and pushed the banana away.

"Wonder why he doesn't eat it?" mused Julian as he watched. "Remember how ravenous Ginny was?"

"I don't think it's because he isn't hungry," said Edie. "Maybe he doesn't trust us. He isn't sure if he should eat it."

"Eric," said Julian, "eat your banana and see if Mark will eat his."

Eric took a bite from his half of the banana, but Mark only watched and shrank farther into his corner of the seat, farther away from the banana Edie held out to him.

"Looks as if he isn't going to eat it," said Edie. "Let's get going and stop soon for milk. Maybe he'll drink that."

In a maze of traffic, the Garths made their way out of the parking lot and onto the crowded highway. When they came to a roadside restaurant, they stopped, and Julian bought a carton of milk with a straw for each boy.

Mark watched Eric put the straw in his mouth and suck. But he continued to sit hunched in his corner of the seat and refused the milk as he had refused the banana.

"Maybe he's never had milk before," said Julian.

"He doesn't look starved," said Edie, "as Ginny did. But food in a crowded orphanage must be pretty skimpy."

When the car stopped in front of the Andersons' house,

Ginny and Angela came tumbling out of the front door and down to the gate.

"Where is he? Where is our new brother? We want to see him!" they clamored.

"Sh-h-h!" cautioned Edie. "Speak gently to him. He can't understand what you're saying, and he's a bit afraid of everybody."

"Why is he afraid?" asked Ginny.

"He doesn't know who we are," Edie told her.

Edie led Mark by one hand toward the Andersons' front door. The others followed. Angela clung to Julian's hand, and Ginny danced along in front of Eric, chattering. Inside the house, Gene sat in Grandpa's lap, patting Tigger.

"Hurry in," said Grandma at the first sight of Mark. "I suspect your boy's starved, and supper's ready."

At the supper table, Mark stared at his food for a time and nibbled at the edges of it.

After supper, Grandma put Gene to bed. While Julian, Eric, Ginny, and Angela sang, Edie held Mark, solemn and still afraid, in her lap.

"Suppose, children," said Julian to Eric, Ginny, and Angela when their bedtime came, "suppose I don't whoo-whoo you to bed tonight. Just tonight. Mark isn't used to that. I'm afraid our noisy whoo-whooing would scare him."

"Why would it scare him, Daddy?" Ginny asked.

"He may not be used to so much noise as we make," said Julian. "And besides, he wouldn't understand what we're doing. Let's go to bed quietly tonight. I'll go with you and tuck you in."

"I might as well put Mark on the floor to begin with," said Edie when the others were tucked in. "He probably has never slept in a bed. Julian, will you spread a blanket for him on the floor in Eric's room?"

Julian spread the blanket and brought pajamas for the newest Garth. When Edie tried to undress Mark, he pushed her hand away and clutched his shirt tightly.

"Wonder what that means," said Grandma.

"Maybe he thinks we're taking his clothes away from him," suggested Julian.

"Then I'll let him sleep in his clothes," said Edie.

She carried Mark to Eric's room and laid him on the blanket. Mark lay quiet for only a minute before he was up and wandering into the living room.

"Let me see if I can make him happy," said Julian. "Where's our kitten, Grandpa?"

"In the kitchen," said Grandpa. "I'll fetch him."

When Grandpa returned from the kitchen with Tigger, Julian lifted Mark in one arm and the kitten in the other.

"Look here, Mark," he said. "Look who's come to say good night to you."

Mark looked at the kitten. He held out his arms for the small animal.

Julian placed Tigger in the boy's hands, but at once Mark squeezed the kitten so firmly that Tigger meowed in pain.

"We must be kind to Tigger, Mark," explained Julian, as he rescued Tigger from the child's grasp. In Eric's room, he laid Mark on the blanket once more. Then he lay down beside him, gathered Tigger in one arm, and gently rubbed the kitten's fur. Tigger purred.

"Do you want to rub the kitten?" Julian asked. He held Tigger close to Mark.

Again Mark took the kitten in his hands. Soon he was squeezing him again.

"Tigger," said Julian to the kitten, "you've had enough for one night. I think Mark would like to be friends with you, but he doesn't know how. So I'm going to put you back in the kitchen and you can come again another night."

That night Mark slept fitfully on his blanket on the floor. He was up and down, up and down. Edie and Julian spent much of the night trying to comfort him.

Early the following morning the Garths drove home. Edie spent a busy afternoon in and out of the house. She let Eric, Ginny, and Angela go into the yard to play. "Take Mark with you, Eric," she said. "Maybe you can get him to play in the swing with you."

Inside the house, Gene, missing Ginny, cried and refused to be pacified. And hardly were the other children outside in the yard when Eric came tearing into the house.

"Mommie!" he shouted. "Mark's run away!"

"Where has he gone?" Edie started in alarm.

"He ran across the street," said Eric. "Right in front of a car."

Edie hurried out the front door in time to see Mark disappearing behind a neighbor's house. She ran after him and led him back to the Garth yard.

"I hope we don't have to fence this yard," she said. "Eric, do you suppose you could watch Mark and keep him from running away? He doesn't know he belongs here with us and is supposed to stay here. How would you like to be a little watchdog and, whenever you see Mark running away, go after him and bring him back. Can you do that?''

"A little watchdog!" said Eric, beaming. "I'm a little watchdog. Come here, Mark, and we'll play with my ball.''

"Can I be a watchdog, too?" begged Ginny.

"Yes," said Edie. "I'll put Gene outdoors in his basket, and you be a watchdog for him.''

"Who's going to be Angela's watchdog?" asked Ginny.

"You can be her watchdog, too," said Edie. "Is everybody set now?''

The afternoon passed, but for Edie it was a rough one. Julian came home from the university just as Angela burst through the front door, crying and holding a small cart, once with wheels on it but now without.

"Look!" she sobbed. "Look, Daddy!"

Julian took the cart and examined it.

"What happened, Angela?" he asked.

"Mark did it," sobbed Angela. "He took my cart in his hands and smashed it. Like this," she said, crushing the cart between her hands.

"Go and tell Eric to bring Mark here," Julian told her.

Julian took the cart in his hands.

"Mark," he said, "it's better—lots better—to build than to destroy. Let's put these wheels back on the cart. Ginny, please ask your Mommie to send me the glue out of the drawer in the kitchen.''

Ginny ran for the glue. When she brought it, Julian carefully replaced three of the wheels.

He put glue on the fourth wheel and handed it to Mark.

Mark, puzzled, took the wheel in his right hand. Julian placed the cart in his left.

"Now, put the wheel on the cart," Julian told him.

Mark looked at Julian. The puzzled expression was still on his face.

"You can do it!" Julian encouraged him.

Timidly Mark put the wheel in place on the cart. He looked up at Julian inquiringly.

"There!" said Julian. "Aren't we proud now! We'll put the cart on the windowsill. Don't play with it till morning, Angela. Give the glue time to dry."

In the days that followed, Mark tore up Ginny's doll house, her doll furniture, and her doll. He tore up Eric's toy train. He tore up almost anything he could lay his hands on. Though he seemed to want to be friends with Tigger, he hurt the kitten often.

Every evening Mark watched the other children getting into their beds, but he continued to sleep on a blanket on the floor. Every night before he lay down, he went looking for Tigger.

One night after the children were in bed, Julian sat in the living room reading the evening paper. Tigger lay in his lap, sleeping. Mark, in his pajamas, wandered into the room.

"Come and rub Tigger's back, Mark," Julian said. "Like this." Julian stroked the kitten gently.

Mark understood nothing of what his father was saying, but he saw what his father was doing. He placed a hand on Tigger's back and stroked the kitten gently. Then he pulled Tigger's tail, hard.

"That hurts Tigger, Mark," Julian told him. "But he likes for you to rub him. Rub him again."

Julian stroked Tigger and Mark stroked him.

"How would you like for Tigger to lie on your blanket beside you?" asked Julian. "Here." Julian carried Mark into the bedroom, lay down on the blanket, nestled Tigger beside him, and stroked the kitten gently. Mark squatted beside Julian and he, too, stroked the kitten.

"Lie down here," said Julian, pointing to the space on the other side of Tigger.

For a moment Mark looked at the space. Then he lay down and nestled Tigger in the crook of his arm. While Tigger purred, Mark fell fast asleep.

"Mommie," reported Julian as he came out of the boys' bedroom and closed the door behind him, "I believe Mark has at last learned how to treat something he loves."

Every night after that Mark, at bedtime, went looking for Tigger. He no longer pulled the kitten's tail nor squeezed him.

One evening, at bedtime, Mark, with Tigger in his arms, stood looking at Eric lying in his bed. He looked at his own bed and at his blanket on the floor. Slowly he climbed into his bed, and, after a time, fell asleep.

At bedtime each evening Mark watched Julian whoo-whoo the other children to their beds.

"Want me to whoo-whoo you to bed, too, Mark?" Julian asked one evening as he came back to the living room after whoo-whooing the other children to bed.

Over Mark's face spread a slow grin.

"Come on, then. Lie down on the floor," Julian said, beckoning to Mark with his finger.

Slowly, with the grin still on his face, Mark lay down on the floor close to Julian. Julian picked him up by the ankles, carried him head downward into his bedroom, and dropped him into bed.

"Now," he said, looking down at Mark and smiling, "didn't you like that?"

Mark smiled shyly up at him.

"Wait!" said Julian. "We forgot something, didn't we?"

He hurried out of the room and returned shortly with Tigger in his arms. He placed the kitten beside Mark. Mark put one arm around Tigger, and, while Tigger purred, Mark fell asleep.

"We're making headway," Julian said later to Edie that evening, as they stood looking at the sleeping boy lovingly holding the sleeping kitten in the crook of his arm.

6

And Julie

"You know," said Julian to Edie one evening in September after Ginny had started kindergarten and Eric had become a first grader, "we need one more girl. We have three boys and two girls, and, to even things up, we should have one more girl."

Edie was pinning a diaper on Gene.

"Are you serious?" she asked, looking up.

"In this house we have room for one more," Julian said. "Don't you think it would be nice to have the same number of boys and girls? If we could find a girl younger than Gene by about a couple of years—"

"That means we'd have a brand new baby," said Edie. "Six children! Six mouths to feed!"

"Six heads to educate!" Julian took up the chant.

"Six sets of teeth to straighten!" they chanted together.

"Six sets of clothes to launder! Arguments to settle! Cuts to bandage! Mumps! Sore throats!"

They both laughed.

"With the sixth," said Julian, "our family will be finished. Do you agree? Three boys and three girls? Perfect!"

"I remember when you thought two boys and two girls would be perfect—two children of our own plus two adopted," Edie reminded him.

"We learn as we grow older," Julian told her.

"So far," said Edie, "we've managed with one more than two plus two. Shall we write to the people at the agency Angela and Gene came from and tell them what's on our minds? They always seem to have a child that's meant exactly for us."

"Maybe we should talk it over with the children first," suggested Julian. "They're old enough now to have opinions on the subject."

Edie smiled. "I can hear their opinions now," she said. "Especially Ginny's."

At the supper table, Edie said to Julian, "You tell them."

"Kids," said Julian.

The children looked up from their plates, even Mark, who was beginning to understand English and to speak a few words. They knew from the tone of their father's voice that he was about to say something important. They held forks and spoons in midair and looked at Julian.

"How would you like a sister?" he asked.

"I've got two sisters," said Eric.

"But I mean another one," Julian explained. "I'm talking now about a baby sister. A little baby sister. Two years younger than Gene, maybe.''

"Yippee!''

"When's she coming?''

"Can I go with you to get her?''

"Is she coming in an airplane?''

"What's her name?''

"Can I hold her?''

The questions came fast.

Edie laughed at the eagerness of the children.

"We don't know the answers to your questions because we haven't yet tried to find a little girl such as we want. But if you'd like to have a baby sister, we'll begin looking.''

"Are you going to write a letter?'' asked Eric.

"I'm going to put the letter in the mailbox,'' said Ginny. "Can't I, Mommie? And I'm going to hold the baby when he comes.''

"She,'' corrected Edie. "Remember, this is to be a little girl.''

On Saturday, Edie wrote the agency that the Garths had decided they would like another baby girl—a very young baby girl—even younger than Angela was when she came to them.

The children stood about Edie as she wrote. When the letter was finished and in its envelope, Ginny, with Eric at her heels, raced with it to the mailbox on the corner. Angela and Mark followed closely. Gene howled because they had left him behind. At the mailbox Ginny waited for him.

"Eric,'' she said, "you hold the box open and we'll let Gene drop the letter inside. Everybody look now.''

"See!'' Ginny told Gene as he dropped the letter in the

box. "We're going to have a new baby and you won't be the baby anymore."

Two days later the superintendent of the agency telephoned in response to Edie's letter.

Yes, she said, the agency had a little girl who was exactly what the Garths wanted. It also had a little boy the same age. Didn't the Garths want both of them?

"Oh," Edie explained, "one at a time is all we can manage. And we've decided one more little girl is the limit to our family. Six children are all we can adequately care for."

"Aw, Mommie!" complained Angela.

"We can take another," said Eric. "We can always take one more."

"We'll drive down some Sunday soon and see the little girl," Edie told the superintendent.

"Can I go, too?"

"Mommie, can't I go this time? I didn't get to go last time."

The voices at Edie's elbow were insistent.

When Edie hung up the receiver she turned to the five children standing about her.

"If all of you go, all five of you, plus your father and me, we'll hardly have room for a little baby," she said. "When the time comes, we'll decide who will go with us to see the little girl and who will stay with Grandma and Grandpa. Okay? And," she added, "when we get another baby, I think we'll have to buy a bus to take us places. Else somebody's going to have to stay home."

"Not me!" rose a chorus of children's voices.

That night Edie and Julian decided on a Sunday shortly before Christmas to go to see the baby. "She'll be another Christmas baby," said Julian, "like Angela."

Before the Sunday arrived, however, the Garths had a phone call from the superintendent of an agency in the city in which they lived.

She had heard, said the superintendent, that the Garths were interested in adopting another child. A baby. The mother of a baby to be born soon had already signed papers releasing the baby to the agency for adoption. Wouldn't the Garths like to adopt the baby, the superintendent asked.

"We're looking for a baby girl," Edie explained. "We've decided to take one more girl to round out our family."

"If it's a little girl, I'll call you," said the superintendent.

At suppertime, Edie told the Garths about her telephone conversation.

"Which baby should it be?" she asked. "The baby already born or the baby that's going to be born? Provided, of course," she added, "the one that hasn't been born turns out to be a girl?"

"Both!" shouted Ginny.

Edie sighed. "We ought to be a dozen homes," she said. "Then we could take six dozen babies."

"If we were a hundred homes we could take six hundred babies," said Eric.

"Good for your arithmetic, Eric!" praised Julian. "But," he slumped in his chair, "I don't feel quite equal to six hundred children. Or even one hundred."

"If we had even half a hundred, we'd look like a baby factory," said Edie.

"What's a factory?" Mark wanted to know.

"It's where a lot of people work together to make things," Edie explained.

"Isn't that what we are?" asked Ginny. "A baby factory? We work together. And we get lots of babies."

"We work together most of the time," said Julian, with a sideward glance at Ginny.

"I told the superintendent at the agency here that we wanted to see the little girl at the other agency," said Edie, "and after we had seen her we'd decide."

The Sunday on which Edie and Julian were to drive to the out-of-town agency arrived. Snow arrived with it. When the Garths awoke, they looked out on a city covered with snow, deep and cold, and piled high against buildings where it had drifted in the night.

Julian stepped outside. Inside again, he reported, "The snow's piled so high against the garage that it would take an hour of shoveling to get the door open and the car out. And after that, there's no telling what the roads will be like. So the trip is off for today."

"Then we can get the baby here," Ginny said.

"Today. This morning," said Angela.

"The baby hasn't even been born yet, Angela," Edie told her. "And until it is, we won't know if it's a girl."

"I don't believe I have another free day to drive to the agency out of town before the end of January," said Julian. "So we may have to let circumstances decide for us whether we take the baby there or the baby here."

"In a way I feel committed to the baby there," said Edie. "I wonder—"

She turned to the children. "Whose turn is it to set the table?" she asked.

"Eric's," said Ginny. "I set it last time."

"Then you come along, Ginny, and help me with breakfast," said Edie. "You come, too, Mark. Angela, you can help Eric. Julian will help Gene get his shoes on."

On a stormy night in early January the phone rang and Julian answered it.

"Oh?" the other Garths heard him say. And, after a moment, "Suppose I have Edie talk with you."

"Is it a baby?" the children asked in hushed tones, dancing around Julian while listening to Edie.

At the other end of the line the superintendent of the local agency was saying, "The baby has come and it's just what you ordered. A little girl. She's a beautiful little black baby and would fit right into your household."

"There's one drawback," added the superintendent. "She was born prematurely and must stay in an incubator for a few weeks. When she weighs five pounds, the hospital will release her."

"Well," said Edie, "it looks as if she'll be needing a home possibly more than the other child we had in mind. So let us know when she has been released from the hospital."

When Edie hung up the receiver, she was surrounded by the children, all of them asking questions.

"What did she say, Mommie? What did she say?"

"It's a girl," Edie told him.

"Goody! Goody!"

"What's her name, Mommie?"

"When will we get her? Tomorrow?"

Edie explained to them why they would not be able to take the baby right away. She turned to Julian.

"Do you think I did right, deciding to take this one instead of the other?"

"A little child needing a home is a little child needing a home, no matter who or where she is," Julian told her. "And maybe somebody else will take the other little girl."

"Why can't we take both little girls?" asked Ginny. "I'll help take care of them."

"You're going to be in first grade next fall, Ginny, and will be in school all day," Edie reminded her. "So you can't help a great deal because you won't be here. Anyway, we're already like the old woman in the Mother Goose rhyme whose shoe was filled with children. We'll all have to move over a bit to make room for one more."

"What's her name?" asked Angela.

"What would you like to name her?" asked Edie.

Angela thought. "Uh-uh-uh—"

"How would you like to name her Julie?" asked Edie. "Do you like that name? She could be named for your father, Julian."

Angela nodded.

"Julie! That's a good name," decided Ginny.

"I think so, too," said Julian.

"All right," said Edie. "Julie she'll be."

One morning, while the Garths still waited for their new baby, Edie awoke with a very sore throat. Directly after breakfast, the superintendent telephoned to say that the baby at last weighed five pounds and the hospital was releasing her the next day.

"Oh, dear!" sighed Edie. She told the superintendent about her sore throat. "I wouldn't dare bring the baby into the house now. Could you care for her at the agency until my throat is well?" she asked.

"Don't worry about the baby," said the superintendent. "We'll put her for a while in a foster home. We have a very good one for taking babies that need care for only a few days."

On a wintry March afternoon following a thaw, Edie telephoned the superintendent that she was well and the Garths were ready for the baby. "We've named her Julie," she said.

Later that afternoon, after Eric and Ginny were home from school, a car turned into the Garths' driveway and stopped. In it were two women. One was the driver of the car. The other held a small bundle in her arms.

At sight of the car, the young Garths let out a whoop, flung the front door wide, and rushed out to the car. Edie followed them.

As soon as the woman holding the bundle stepped out of the car, the children surrounded her.

"Let me see! Let me see!" they chorused, tugging at the blanket in which the baby was bundled.

"Children, stand back," said Edie. "Let's not unwrap the baby till we're inside. It's too cold out here."

When all were in the house, Edie took the bundle from the woman. The children crowded around her. Edie turned back the blanket. In it lay a tiny black child with slim fingers curled into tight little fists.

"She weighs six pounds now," said the woman.

"She's as tiny as Angela's doll," said Eric.

"And, look!" said Ginny. "She hasn't got any eye-lashes!"

"She will grow some," said the woman. "She only needs a little time."

When the women had gone, Angela asked, "Can I hold the baby, Mommie?"

"I want to hold her," said Ginny. "I'm older than Angela."

"Well, I'm older than you, Ginny," said Eric. "Let me hold her first, Mommie."

"All of you sit down on the floor," said Edie. "Each of you may hold Julie one minute. Angela asked first, so she may hold her first."

The children sat in a circle on the floor and Edie laid the tiny baby in Angela's lap. "While you hold Julie, I'll bring the basket that I've lined for her," she said, "and when you have all held her, we'll put her in that."

When Ginny's turn came to hold the baby, Gene began to cry.

"What's the matter, honey?" Ginny asked.

For reply, Gene got up from the floor and tried to crowd into Ginny's lap along with the baby.

"Look, Gene," said Ginny. "You're a big boy now. And you've got a little sister, see? I'll have to take care of her but you're big enough to take care of yourself."

Gene continued to cry.

"See, Gene," Ginny consoled him. "You sit here on the floor beside me and you can hold Julie's feet in your lap while I hold her head in mine. Okay?"

"Okay," whimpered Gene, wiping his eyes with his sleeve.

Edie returned with the basket and set it on the floor. Tigger followed her.

"Have all of you held Julie?" she asked. "If you have, we'll put her in the basket and let her sleep. She needs lots of sleep. Sleep will help her grow."

"And will she really get some eyelashes?" asked Ginny anxiously.

"She will," Edie assured Ginny. "Just give her time."

She laid the baby gently in the basket and hurried to the kitchen. The children crowded around the basket. Tigger wormed his way among them.

"Tigger wants to see her, too," said Mark. "All right," he said, lifting Tigger up. "Look."

Tigger looked, purred, and looked until Mark put him down beside the basket.

"Look at Tigger!" screamed Angela suddenly.

While no one was watching, Tigger had perched on the rim of the basket and was preparing to nestle inside.

Angela grabbed him and spanked him.

"Angela!" scolded Mark. "Don't spank so hard."

Edie came hurrying into the room. "What's this commotion about?" she asked.

The children, all talking at once, told her about the cat.

"He's a mean kitty," said Angela.

"No, Tigger's not mean," Mark defended the kitten. "You wanted to see the baby, didn't you? Well, Tigger wanted to see her too."

"No," said Edie. "Tigger's not really mean. He just thinks the basket would be a nice soft place for taking a nap.

Mark," she added, "you sit here beside the basket and keep
Tigger away from the baby."

Mark gathered Tigger in his arms and sat beside the
basket, gently rubbing the kitten's back.

"I know!" shouted Angela. "We'll take turns watching."

"That's a good idea," agreed Edie. "Mark watches
first."

"What will we do at night when we're all asleep?"
asked Mark.

"I'll put the basket beside my bed," Edie told him,
"and cover it with netting. Then Tigger can't get in."

"How long does Mark get to watch?" asked Eric.

"Five minutes," said Edie. "Tonight I'll excuse all of

you from helping me with supper and let you watch Julie instead. You can take turns watching five minutes each.''

''I can tell time,'' said Eric. ''I'll be timekeeper.''

The children seated themselves on the floor, with Mark
nearest the basket. Now and then he pulled back the blanket
and took a peep at Julie.

''You'll wake her,'' scolded Ginny, taking a peep, too.

''I had to see if she's breathing,'' said Mark. ''She's so
little you can hardly tell.''

There, quietly, they sat around the basket, Eric and
Ginny and Angela and Gene, as Mark watched Julie and
Eric watched the clock. Gene got up from the floor and
crowded into Ginny's lap.

''Gene,'' Ginny bargained, ''if I let you sit in my lap

while I watch Julie, will you let me watch her your five minutes, too?''

"Okay," agreed Gene.

Quietly they sat.

Gene looked up at Ginny and smiled. "Let's do this every day," he suggested.

7

And Peter

One Saturday morning in October the postman delivered a letter to the Garths from a welfare agency in Illinois.

Edie looked at the letter suspiciously. She showed the return address to Julian. "I wonder how many children these people have for us?" she mused.

"Remember," said Julian, "we wrote them once and asked if they had any children of mixed parentage for adoption?"

"They said they had nothing to offer us. Remember?" asked Edie.

"Well," said Julian, "I suspect they have the ideal baby for us now."

"Oh, no, they haven't," said Edie stoutly.

"Shall we open the letter and see?" suggested Julian.

"Before you open it," warned Edie, "brace yourself so

you won't be tempted. Remember we have six children already."

"Six mouths to feed!" began Julian.

"Six heads to educate!" Edie joined in. "Six sets of teeth to straighten! Six sets of clothes to launder! Arguments to settle! Cuts to bandage! Mumps! Sore throats!" They both laughed.

"But we can love one more, can't we?" asked Julian, fingering the letter.

"We can love one more long distance," said Edie, "but not adopt one more."

"Anyway," said Julian, "let's find out what they're offering."

He tore open the envelope, took the letter out, and read it aloud to Edie.

" 'Dear Mr. and Mrs. Garth,' it says. 'Some time ago you wrote us regarding the adoption of a child of mixed parentage. At that time we had no such child in our care. Now, however, we do have such a child, and we think he would be ideal for you.' "

"Didn't I tell you?" asked Edie.

Julian scanned the lines in the letter. He cleared his throat.

"Listen to this, Edie," he said, his voice tinged with excitement. " 'He is a little Mexican-American boy, ten months old, whom we have not been able to place in a home for adoption. Unless we can place him soon, we shall have to put him in a foster home. Then, until he is in his teens and able somehow to fend for himself, he will be shunted from foster home to foster home. And that, as you know, is not a happy way for any child to grow up.' "

"Anything more?" asked Edie.

Julian read further from the letter.

" 'He is a lovely little boy, and, because we are very anxious to place him in a home such as yours, we hope you will consider adopting him.' "

Edie was quiet for a moment.

"We can think about all our friends," she said, "and see if we can recommend any couple who want to adopt a child and who might meet the needs of this little boy."

"Oh, I don't know," said Julian.

"What?"

Edie looked hard at Julian, her eyes wide with suspicion.

"What did you say?" she asked.

"Well," Julian hesitated. "Remember back in Texas—"

"That was a long time and six children ago," Edie reminded him.

"But we haven't forgotten," said Julian. "Remember how we talked about adopting two Mexican-American children? Just Mexican-American children and nobody else? And then we moved away and under all the pressures I sort of forgot them. No," he corrected himself, "I never really forgot them. I couldn't. They were such lovable children— so warm, and friendly, and full of life and fun. And here is one being offered us for the taking."

"Practically set down in our laps," amended Edie.

"And, look," said Julian, pointing to the pages on which information about the little boy was written. "He was born almost on my birthday. His birthday is just one day from mine."

"That's no argument," teased Edie. "Remember we already have one child almost the age of this one. Julie. Her birthday is only six days from yours. If we took this Mexican-American child we'd practically have twins. They were born just one week apart."

Edie took the letter from Julian and glanced down the page quickly. "You know, Julian," she said, "twins just might be fun." She hesitated. "But *seven* mouths to feed! Let's sleep on this one, good and hard," she suggested.

They did sleep on it. For a week they said little about it. During the week Julian seemed strangely quiet. Into his eyes came a brooding look while Edie, herself, felt deeply stirred by the memories of the Mexican-American children with whom she had once worked.

"I can't explain exactly why," said Julian, "but I feel as if I'm betraying somebody if we don't take this boy. I feel as if he's my own little boy and he needs me to love him. Besides," he added, "we need him to love. Something's missing from our lives unless we take him."

One evening, when the children were in bed, Edie said to Julian, "I have a confession to make, Julian. I think I'm beginning to feel as you do about that child."

"You honestly feel that way, Edie?" Julian asked. "After all, the work falls mainly on you. I can earn the money to fill the children's stomachs and educate their heads, and even to pay for straightening the teeth that will need straightening. But the rest—the laundry, the arguments, the cuts, the mumps, the sore throats—all these will fall mainly on you. And maybe that's more than you ought to undertake."

"I've decided there's nothing more valuable I could be doing," Edie said. "No," she reassured him, "I think I'm beginning to feel a real responsibility for this particular child. Just as you do. So will you write the agency to get things underway? Or shall I?"

"You're sure, Edie?" Julian pressed her.

"Yes, I'm sure. Quite sure," Edie insisted.

He kissed her tenderly.

"Suppose I write this letter," he said. "Somehow, deep down, there's something very special to me about this child. It's as if—as if, at last I'm keeping a promise I made to Mexican-American children—and to myself—a long, long time ago."

It was not until Thanksgiving that Julian and Edie found time to go for the baby. In the early afternoon of Thanksgiving Day, the eight Garths loaded into the minibus they had just acquired, and started for the Andersons' house. On the way Edie taught the children to sing "To Grandmother's House We Go."

"Is riding in a car different from riding in a sleigh?" asked Eric.

"Boy, you discover the difference quickly, I can tell you," said Julian. "Of course, to ride in a sleigh you have to have snow, so that the horses can pull the sleigh along on its runners. And all the time the horses' sleighbells go jingle, jingle, jingle. But snow means cold wind blowing into your faces and making your eyes smart and sting. In a car you can keep snug and warm. How would you really rather go to Grandma's—in a car or in a sleigh?"

"A sleigh! A sleigh!" came a loud chorus of votes from

the back of the minibus where each child had been assigned a seat and was securely strapped in.

"We'll see if we can find somebody to take us on a sleigh ride someday," promised Julian. "Or some night. Night is when a sleigh ride is the most fun. But first we'll have to have a big snow on the ground. Right now we have something more exciting than a sleigh ride to talk about. Your mother and I have something to tell you," he added. "Something very important. You tell them, Edie."

Edie turned in the front seat of the minibus to face the children.

"Tomorrow, children, your father and I are going to Illinois, and we're going to bring back a little brother for you."

"Wowee!"

"Can I go too, Mommie?"

"What's his name?"

"How big is he?"

Questions exploded from the back seats.

"Your father and I have named him Peter," Edie told the children. "He's ten months old. And we've decided Angela and Mark may go with us to bring him back to Grandma's."

"Whoopee!" came from Angela and Mark, while from the others there was a muffled, "Aw, shucks, Mommie! Why can't I go?"

It was still dark the morning after Thanksgiving when Edie roused Mark and Angela.

Mark was hard to wake up on any morning. That morning, after having eaten Grandma's big Thanksgiving dinner the evening before, he seemed unusually hard to wake up.

"Mark! Mark!" Edie called as she shook him. "Remember we're going for your little brother today."

At the word "brother," Mark opened his eyes drowsily and let them fall shut again. Suddenly he opened them wide and sat upright in bed. Then he yawned and fell back on his pillow.

"It's dark," he complained.

"I know it's dark," Edie told him. "But we have a long way to go. If we're going to get your baby brother and bring him back to Grandma's tonight, we have to start now."

Yawning and stretching, Mark rolled out of bed and began pulling on his clothes.

"Ready, Mommie," called Angela from another room.

"Sh-h-h!" warned Edie. "Don't wake the other children."

Quietly the four of them, Julian and Edie, Mark and Angela, closed the door behind them, got into the minibus, and set out down the highway.

"Hey, look!" cried Mark, suddenly coming to life. "Stars! Stars in the morning! Do they stay there all night?"

"They stay there all the time," Julian told him.

"Then why can't I see them all the time?" Mark wanted to know.

"Because the sun is brighter than the stars," Julian explained. "You keep your eyes on the stars and see how bright the sun must be to fade them out."

As they drove along in the early dawn, the four of them watched the stars fade from sight, at first one by one, later, suddenly it seemed, all together.

It was past noon when the Garths reached the welfare agency. They were warmly welcomed by the superintendent and a nurse. Inside, they sat down to talk about the little Mexican-American boy and to discuss the papers that had to be signed before the Garths could take the child across the state line. Mark grew restless. They talked too long, he thought.

"When can I see my new brother?" he asked.

"Just a few more minutes now," the superintendent promised. "We've almost finished with these papers."

At last the nurse went for the little boy.

"We're calling him Peter," Edie told the superintendent.

"Peter," repeated the superintendent. "A fine name. And are his brother and sister here going to help take care of him?" he asked, turning to Angela and Mark.

"I can feed him," volunteered Angela.

"Can he catch frogs?" asked Mark.

Everybody laughed. "Not yet, Mark," said Julian. "He's just a little boy, remember. Give him time to grow up and then he'll help you catch frogs."

Finally the nurse returned, carrying the child. She sat down and placed him on her lap. Angela crowded close and held his hand. Mark watched from a distance.

Julian took the child in his arms, placed him on his shoulder, and patted him gently on the back.

"At last, Peter," he said, "we've got together, you and I." He lowered the child and looked at him intently. "Exactly right," he said. "Dark brown eyes, black hair."

"What's best," said the superintendent, "he's a bubbly little boy, a boy everybody has to love. You'll soon find that out."

"Well," said Edie in a businesslike tone of voice, "if

we're to get back to Grandma's tonight, we'd better finish up here and get started. I brought some clothes for Peter. Bring him here, Julian, and I'll put them on. I think they'll fit an eleven-month-old.''

Quickly Edie took off the clothes Peter was wearing and put on those she had brought.

"Did you bring shoes?" the nurse asked.

"I never put shoes on my children until they begin to walk," explained Edie.

"But he's walking already," said the nurse. "He walks everywhere."

"At eleven months?" asked Edie.

"Let him walk now," begged Angela. She took the child's hand. "Come, Peter," she said. "Let's see you walk."

Edie stood Peter on the floor. Angela took one hand. Mark hurried to take the other. Across the floor walked the three, Peter tottering along between Angela and Mark.

"See!" exclaimed Mark, looking back at his father and smiling. "I'll bet he can catch frogs."

"Maybe," agreed Julian. "When they begin croaking in the spring, we'll see."

"I'll tell you what," said the nurse. "We'll let him keep the shoes he has on. They'll last a while longer, and you won't have to buy new ones right away."

In the early afternoon the Garths climbed into the minibus. Edie held Peter on her lap.

"Can't we have him back here, Mommie?" begged Mark.

"Suppose I hold him till he gets a bit used to us," said Edie. "Then I'll wrap him up and strap him on the middle

seat back of us. You two can sit on the seat back of him and watch over him. Sit down now and fasten your seat belts.''

"I think we ought to celebrate this great occasion,'' said Julian as they drove along. "I noticed a Pancake House in the next town. How about pancakes for everybody?''

"Yippee!'' shouted Mark and Angela from the back seat. Mark licked his lips noisily. "Pancakes!'' he said. "I'm going to have— I'm going to have—what kind of pancakes are you going to have, Angela? I'm going to have peanut butter pancakes, and blueberry pancakes, and strawberry pancakes, and—and—potato pancakes, and pancakes with little pigs rolled in them, and—''

When the minibus reached the Pancake House, Mark and Angela clambered noisily out.

"Is Peter going to eat pancakes, too?'' asked Angela, as Julian stepped out, took Peter from Edie, and held the door open for her.

"Peter isn't big enough yet for pancakes,'' explained Edie. "I have some milk for him.''

"Aw, Mommie,'' complained Mark. "He's big enough for pancakes. Anybody that can walk is big enough for pancakes.''

"I'll give him a good supper when we get to Grandma's,'' Edie promised.

The feast of the pancakes was a noisy celebration. Peter drank his milk as Mark and Angela sampled four different kinds of syrup on their pancakes and tasted Edie's and Julian's pancakes with still other kinds of syrup.

When they had finished, they got into the minibus once more. Peter was fast asleep.

"I'm sleepy, too,'' yawned Mark.

"I don't wonder," said Edie. "You and Angela stretch out on the back seat and go to sleep. I'll strap Peter in the middle seat."

"Who's going to watch him?" asked Mark.

"I will," said Edie. "I won't let anything happen to him."

Mark and Angela lay down, one at either end of the back seat. Edie strapped them in, and covered them with a blanket. Julian started the car.

Soon all was quiet in the back seat.

"Guess what, Mommie?" Mark broke the silence. "Next time we go to get a baby, I'm going to have forty kinds of pancakes."

Julian chuckled.

"Mark," he said, "there isn't going to be a next time. This is the last baby the Garths are going to get."

"Aw, shucks!" muttered Mark as he pulled the blanket over his shoulders.

After a while he roused and propped his chin in the palm of his hand.

"This isn't the last baby we're going to get, is it, Mommie?" he asked.

"You heard what your daddy said," Edie told him. "I think this is the last one. But when we got you, I thought you were the last one. And now we have two more. I'm beginning to think we'll just have to wait and see if somewhere, sometime, somebody hasn't a baby waiting just for us."

8

And, Finally, Emily

One morning, late in spring, just after Edie had finished giving Peter and Julie their baths, the phone rang.

"I have news for you," said Julian when Edie answered.

"What is it?" asked Edie. "You sound excited."

"How would you like to live in North Carolina?"

"North Carolina!" exclaimed Edie. "It sounds warm and sunny after this cold winter we've had here. When are we moving? This morning?" Then, in a more serious voice, she asked, "What's all this about?"

"I've just had a letter," Julian told her, "asking me to come to North Carolina this fall to teach in a university there."

"And you're going?" asked Edie.

"That's for you to help decide," said Julian. "The head

of the communications department wants me to come down soon to talk things over.''

''Do you think North Carolina is ready for this crew of ours?'' Edie asked.

''This crew of ours would take North Carolina by storm,'' declared Julian. ''Do you suppose you could go with me to look the situation over?''

''Go with you? Not now,'' said Edie after a moment's hesitation. ''Seven children are too much for Grandma and Grandpa to take care of while we'd be gone, even with a field full of broccoli. Anyway, the children mustn't be taken out of school. So you plan to go alone. Whatever you decide will be fine with me.''

While Julian was away, Edie found time for reading each evening after the children were in bed. One evening, an article in a magazine caught her eye. It was about Vietnamese children.

Thousands of American soldiers were fighting and dying in a war in Vietnam, said the article. Thousands of Vietnamese soldiers and civilians were being killed. Hundreds of homes were being bombed and burned to ashes, and Vietnamese people were streaming along the roads, carrying a few belongings on their heads and on their backs, trying to find places where they would be safe from bombs.

Most pitiful among the homeless people, said the article, were the children. The fathers and mothers of many of them had been killed, and fire had been set to their homes. The children seemed to belong to nobody. They straggled along the roads, crying, afraid, hungry. Some of them were

fortunate enough to reach a town where there was an orphanage to take care of homeless children. But the orphan-
ages were so crowded that no more children could be got inside. Children who couldn't get in were left to wander, to
eat from garbage dumps when they could find garbage
dumps, and to sleep wherever they were when they could no
longer stay awake, often beside a road or on a sidewalk.
Some children slept beside pigs to keep warm—whenever
they could find pigs.

Edie thought of little else than the Vietnamese orphans
the rest of the time Julian was away.

When Julian came home, he announced that the Garths
would go to live in North Carolina early in September. He
liked the teaching offer the university had made him. He
liked the university, the town, and the people. He had gone
house hunting and had found a house for the Garth family—a big green house, set in a big shady yard on a street
called Hemlock Drive—a yard with a small creek flowing
through the back of it, where the children could wade and
build dams and bridges and listen to frogs and watch minnows darting about in the water.

That evening when all the children were in their beds
and asleep, Edie said to Julian, "We must add one more
child to our family before we go to North Carolina."

"One more child? What are you talking about?" asked
Julian.

Edie handed Julian the magazine with the article about
the Vietnamese orphans.

"Read this," she said.

Julian hastily read the article.

"Well?" he said.

"Nothing you and I have done has stopped the destruction and the killing and the suffering in Vietnam," said Edie. "We've written to the President. We've gone to Washington and talked with our Senators. We've marched. We've picketed. We've carried signs saying STOP THE WAR. SAVE THE CHILDREN. The killing and the destruction go on. There's still one thing we can do."

"You're not really thinking of adopting another child, are you, Edie?" Julian asked, laying down the magazine and looking straight at her. "With Peter, we have all the children we can care for. I thought we were agreed on that."

"We were," said Edie. "But what's an agreement like ours when you read an article like that? I felt as if somebody was talking straight to me. I can't sleep at night, thinking how safe and happy our seven are and realizing we could all move over a bit and share with one more."

"But, Edie, common sense tells us," Julian said, "that there has to be an end to our family sometime. We're not an orphanage. Eight mouths to feed?"

"Yes," said Edie, "eight mouths to feed. Eight heads to educate. Eight sets of teeth to straighten. Eight sets of clothes to launder. Arguments to settle. Cuts to bandage. Mumps. Sore throats. Everything in the book."

"I'm thinking mainly of you, Edie," said Julian. "You have quite enough to do, taking care of seven children, without adding another."

"Remember how when we got the letter about Peter you said you felt as if he were your own little boy and he needed you to love him and father him?" asked Edie.

"Yes," said Julian, "I remember. I still feel that way."

"That's exactly the way I feel about some little Vietnamese orphan—some little Vietnamese girl," said Edie. "A little girl would even things up. We'd then have four girls and four boys. I can mother one more little daughter, and I can't sleep nights wondering what may be happening to her and where she may be hiding from the bombs. And, remember, the children, especially Eric and Ginny, and even Mark and Angela, give me lots of help now. They save me many a step."

The two sat for several minutes in silence. Finally Julian spoke.

"If that's the way you feel, Edie—I know it's the way I felt about Peter—we'll think about getting a Vietnamese daughter. We must keep doing everything possible to stop the killing and destruction in Vietnam. But I'm sure, by moving over a bit, all of us, we can make room for a Vietnamese orphan. It's the least we can do. Shall we talk it over with the children?"

"Of course," said Edie. "Tomorrow evening."

The next evening, when the books had been read and the songs sung, Edie said, "Children, before you go to bed, your father and I want to talk something over with you."

"Is it about school?"

"Is it about moving to North Carolina?"

"Is it about my birthday?"

"Is it about Christmas?"

Questions came tumbling out.

"It's about something more important than any of these," said Julian, "more important than all of them together," he added. "It's about a new little sister."

"When's she coming?"

"Is she coming in an airplane?"

"Can I go this time to get her?"

"We don't know the answers to your questions yet," said Julian. "You all know that a war is going on in a country named Vietnam. Thousands of children have been killed and thousands more have been left homeless."

"I've read about them," spoke up Eric. "And I've seen pictures of them on TV and in magazines. One had been burned by napalm."

"Would you like to have a little sister from Vietnam?" Edie asked the children.

Eric was the first to reply: "I've been thinking we ought to have one," he said.

"How about the rest of you?" asked Julian. "Would you like to have her? We're a bit crowded, but, if everyone of us moves over just a little, we can make room for her, don't you think?"

"She can sleep with me," offered Ginny.

"When's she coming?"

"What's her name?"

"We don't know when she's coming. And we don't know her name yet," said Julian. "We wouldn't know how to pronounce it if we knew it. So let's give her a name we can all pronounce. What do you suggest?"

Rose. Hazel. Mary. Betsy. Eva. Georgia. Emily. The names came rushing.

"How about Emily?" asked Julian.

"Emily!" shouted Ginny. "Let's call her Emily."

Seven children and two parents went to bed that evening

with a happy picture of one small Vietnamese orphan hazily in their minds.

"There isn't time, Edie," said Julian the next morning, "to get Emily here before we move to North Carolina."

"At least we can get things started," said Edie. "I can write to International Social Service this morning and tell the people there the sort of child we want. A little girl, older than Peter and Julie, younger than Gene."

In August, the Garths moved to North Carolina and began life all over again in the big green house set in the big shady yard on Hemlock Drive. In September, Eric, Ginny, Mark, and Angela started school. In September, too, Edie received a letter from International Social Service. It was a bulky letter and it came in a big envelope. It said that International Social Service had found just the little girl the Garths were looking for—a little Vietnamese girl whose father had been killed in the war. Her mother was too poor to care for the child and had taken her to an orphanage. With the letter came a picture of the child—a picture of a little girl with a sad, sad face.

Edie found a small frame, put the picture in it, and set it on the table in the living room where everyone could see it.

"That makes it seem as if Emily'll be here any day now," Edie commented.

But getting Emily out of Vietnam was not to be simple. When Edie wrote to the United States Immigration Service asking for a visa for Emily so that the child might enter this country, she was informed of a law denying any American home the right to adopt more than two Oriental children. The Garths already had one Chinese and one Korean. They could not, therefore, adopt a Vietnamese, she was told.

"What do we do now?" asked Julian.

"Emily needs us and we need her," said Edie. "It's a stupid law that lets us kill the fathers of these children and then won't let us care for the children themselves."

Edie went to a lawyer who lived in their North Carolina city. He was unable to help her, but he gave her the name of a lawyer in Washington, an immigration lawyer, to whom Edie wrote. The Washington lawyer agreed to help, but he warned Edie a long delay was possible. While Emily waited in the Vietnamese orphanage, the Garths waited on Hemlock Drive. Months and months they waited. The children grew impatient.

Edie wrote to Americans living in Saigon, but they seemed unable to help. Finally, she wrote to one of the North Carolina senators in Washington. Would he introduce a private bill in the Senate, a bill that if passed, would allow Emily to enter the United States?

Back came a letter. Yes, wrote the senator, he would gladly introduce the bill.

In a few days Edie received a copy of the bill. It was an important looking document, printed, and numbered: Bill S 3274. It was called "A Bill for the Relief of a Vietnamese Orphan."

With the bill came a letter from the senator. "It usually takes a year to get such a bill through the Senate," he wrote.

"Why don't you forget Emily and ask the International Social Service to find some other family to adopt her?" friends advised.

That evening Edie told Julian and the children about the letter and the advice she had received.

"Let somebody else have Emily?" The children were outraged. "They can't take her away from us. She's ours."

Still they waited. Months more they waited.

Then, one day early in May, when Edie answered the doorbell, she was handed a cablegram that read: "Saigon. May 3, 1968. 1:27 P.M. Consul states your orphan leaving without further procedures there stop dispatching with three others Northwest Airlines Seattle Philadelphia two three weeks."

In great excitement Edie telephoned Julian at the university. What had happened, they wondered. But again, they had to wait.

In a few days, on a Friday, a letter arrived from Saigon. It explained that, because of a ruling of the United States government, only a certain number of Vietnamese people were allowed to enter the United States each month. The American official who granted the visas for Vietnamese to enter the United States found that he had one visa left for the month of May. Just one. This visa he had granted to Emily. But she would lose it if she did not leave Vietnam before the end of May.

"She's coming!" Edie told Gene and Julie and Peter excitedly as she read the letter. "Emily's coming!" she told Eric, Ginny, Mark, and Angela as they came hurrying from school.

"When?"

"Who told you?"

"Who's going to meet her, Mommie?"

"She's coming!" Edie telephoned the good news to Julian.

"No! Really? After all this waiting! I can hardly believe it," said Julian.

When Julian came rushing into the house, Edie put the letter in his hand. "Read it," she said. "Now we'll have to get ready for her. I imagine we'll have at least two weeks to do that."

But on Sunday night when the phone rang, Edie answered and heard the operator say, "I have a long distance call for Mrs. Edith Garth."

"This is Edith Garth," answered Edie.

"All right, go ahead," said the operator to the person at the other end of the line.

"We've just had word," said a woman's voice, "that the plane bringing your Vietnamese child will arrive in Washington at National Airport late on Tuesday."

"Tuesday? You—you mean a week from Tuesday, don't you?" stammered Edie.

"No," said the woman. "Next Tuesday. The day after tomorrow."

Edie hung up the receiver with a bang and turned to Julian and the children. "Emily's coming Tuesday. Emily! The day after tomorrow!" Her voice trembled with excitement. "We're to meet her late Tuesday afternoon at National Airport in Washington."

The children clustered around Edie.

"Mommie, may I go with you?" asked Eric.

"Me, too," said Ginny.

"I want to go, Mommie. May I go?" begged Mark.

"I'm going, too," said Angela.

"Aw, you and Mark got to go for Peter," complained Eric. "It's somebody else's turn now. It's my turn."

"And mine," Ginny reminded him.

"We can't take all of you," Edie said to them.

"Leave Gene and Julie and Peter home. Leave them with the Donaldsons," suggested Ginny.

"We'll see what the Donaldsons think of that," said Edie. "Right now I must get used to the fact that Emily's really coming. On Tuesday. The day after tomorrow. After all this work to get her here, and all the waiting."

The following day, late in the afternoon, when Julian was still at the university, he found an Associated Press message in his mailbox: "Five Vietnamese children left Saigon this afternoon en route for the United States," it read.

Hastily, he telephoned Edie and gave her the message.

"Now," said Edie, "I really believe it. Hurry home," she urged. "Do you realize we have to be in Washington tomorrow? *Tomorrow!*"

Early the following morning, Julian hustled Gene, Julie, and Peter, all of them only half awake, off to the Donaldsons', who would care for them while the Garths were away.

After gulping down breakfast, Eric and Ginny, Angela and Mark, each with a sleeping bag, and Edie and Julian, scrambled into the minibus and headed toward Washington. On the outskirts of Washington they engaged a room in a motel for the night. Then they drove to the Washington National Airport. At Northwest Airlines they were told Emily's plane was due at eight o'clock in the evening.

"All right, kids," said Julian, "we have four hours. Let's see a bit of Washington."

The six of them climbed into the minibus again and set out.

"Don't you think we ought to go back to the airport?" asked Mark when they had seen the White House.

"It's a long time before the plane is due," Julian assured him.

When they had seen the Capitol, Mark asked, "What if the plane comes in early? Don't you think we'd better go back?"

"Don't worry, Mark. We'll get back in plenty of time," Julian said.

When they had seen the Washington Monument, Mark said, almost in tears, "If we don't go back soon, we're going to miss Emily."

Julian looked at his watch. "There's still lots of time, Mark," he said.

At the Lincoln Memorial, Mark began to cry. "What will Emily do if we're not there to meet her?"

"Mark," said Julian, "we'll never know. Because we're going to be there. As soon as I can find a place to turn around, we'll go straight to the airport."

When they arrived at the airport, they hurried to the gate through which passengers from Emily's plane would pass. They listened closely as the arrival of planes was announced.

"How will we know which is Emily's plane?" asked Mark.

"We'll hear on the loudspeaker the name of the airline,

the flight number, and the gate at which the plane is landing,'' explained Julian.

"How will we know Emily?" asked Angela.

"We'll know her by her picture," said Ginny.

"Wonder if she'll know us," said Angela.

"We'll tell her who we are," said Eric.

Finally, over the loudspeaker system came the announcement the Garths had been waiting to hear.

"There's Emily's plane," said Julian.

"Everybody, here comes Emily!" cried Ginny.

Tense with excitement, the Garths craned their necks as down from the sky swooped a big airplane. It bounced, settled on the runway, and taxied toward the ramp.

Suddenly, the Garths were aware that men with cameras were all about them.

"What are they doing?" Angela asked.

"They've had word, I imagine, that somebody very important is on the plane," explained Edie, "and they're here to take his picture."

"Emily's important," said Eric.

"You're mighty right, Emily's important," Julian said.

People came streaming into the airport from the plane. Some were met by relatives or friends, and greetings were loud and happy. Others hurried through the airport alone.

"Where's Emily?" asked Mark anxiously.

"Emily will be along soon," Edie assured him.

Intently the Garths and the photographers watched the passengers.

Still more people came off the plane, but Emily was not among them.

"Do you think—she missed the plane?" Mark asked anxiously.

"I don't think so," Edie told him. "Just wait."

At last, a young woman carrying a little girl in one arm and leading a small boy by the hand appeared in the doorway of the plane.

"There! There, Mommie! There she is! There's Emily!" chorused the children.

"Mommie! Look at her, Mommie!" cried Ginny, craning her neck to see as the woman and the children approached the Garths. "Why—why, she looks just like me!"

Cameras were suddenly turned on the woman and the two children as Edie and Julian, with Eric and Ginny, Mark and Angela crowding at their heels, pushed through the mass of people.

"We are Julian and Edie Garth," Julian said to the woman. "I believe this is our little girl you are carrying."

"Yes," said the woman. She spoke to the little girl in Vietnamese. "And are these her brothers and sisters?" she asked Julian, smiling at the four young Garths crowding around.

With that the cameras were turned on the Garths.

"Mommie! They've taken Emily's picture and now they're taking ours!" exclaimed Ginny. "Are we the important people?"

"Could be," said Edie.

"Of course you're important," Julian told her. "There aren't many families like ours that have an orphan from Vietnam come to join them."

Ginny turned toward the cameras and smiled broadly.

While the photographers collected the names of the children from the woman and Julian, a stewardess said to Edie, "I am going to arrange for a room where you can talk and exchange the necessary papers belonging to your new daughter."

She disappeared in the crowd and, soon afterward, reappeared.

"Follow me," she said as she led the way to a conference room. "You may talk here as long as you like," she said. "No one will disturb you."

Inside the room, the Garth children watched as the woman gave Julian important papers belonging to Emily. Emily whined and clutched the woman's skirt whenever Edie came near her.

When all the business was finished, the woman explained that she was taking the little boy on to Philadelphia and must catch another plane. As Emily watched them leave, she started to whimper. When she could no longer see them, she began to sob.

"There, there, Emily! Don't cry!" Ginny said soothingly as she knelt in front of the unhappy child. "See what I brought you!" She held a small doll toward Emily.

Emily wanted none of the doll. She screamed her anxiety at being left behind with strange people.

"Well," said Julian, lifting Emily in his arms, "we might as well get this over with."

The other Garth children hovered about Emily as Julian made his way through the airport to the lot where the minibus was parked. All the while, Emily screamed her fright and rage.

The Garths climbed into their bus. In the middle seat, Edie tried to hold Emily on her lap. Angela and Ginny sat on either side of her. Emily refused to sit on Edie's lap. She refused to be lifted by Ginny, who offered her the doll again, or by Angela. Instead, she stood on the floor of the bus, clinging to the back of the front seat. As the bus made its way along Washington's crowded streets toward their motel, she screamed her fright and loneliness.

"Poor little thing!" said Ginny, herself almost in tears.

"What makes her cry like that?" asked Mark.

"She doesn't know us," explained Julian. "And she doesn't know where we're taking her."

"You'll be all right, Emily," said Mark, turning in the front seat to comfort her. "You'll learn. You'll be fine."

But Emily would not be comforted. When the Garths arrived at their motel, Emily was so tired from crying that she could only whimper.

"Here, Emily," said Edie, "maybe you'd like some water."

Emily grasped the glass Edie offered and gulped the water down.

"Now," said Edie, "here's a banana I brought for you."

She peeled the banana and handed half of it to Emily. That, too, Emily gulped down.

"We're making headway," said Julian. "She's quit crying, at least."

"Now it's time we eat the sandwiches I brought and get to bed," said Edie. "We've had a big day. We'd better get a good rest and prepare for what's coming tomorrow."

"What's coming?" asked Eric.

"We're going home," said Edie. "And little by little, we'll get Emily used to us so she won't be afraid of us."

When their sandwiches were eaten, the children opened their sleeping bags and spread them on the floor.

"Can Emily sleep in my sleeping bag with me, Mommie?" begged Ginny.

"I brought a sleeping bag for her, too," said Edie. "I'll put it between your sleeping bag and our bed. Before long, I suspect, Emily will want to be carried to her own bed by her heels, the way the rest of you are. One of these days soon," she added, looking at Mark and Eric, "two boys I know are going to be too big to be carried to bed by their heels."

"I think we'll just start that program tonight," said Julian. "I'm dead tired. Eric and Mark," he added, "as of tonight I declare you to be big boys! And Ginny," he added, winking at her, "you're a big girl now. Okay?"

Ginny grinned at her father. With that she, Eric, and Mark crawled into their sleeping bags and were soon fast asleep.

Edie spread Emily's sleeping bag on the floor, but for several minutes Emily only stared at it. After all the other Garths were in bed or in their sleeping bags, and the light was turned out, Emily lay down on her sleeping bag beside Ginny. When she fell asleep, Edie covered her.

Watching the child in the dim light, Edie whispered to Julian, "We're making progress fast."

The next morning, Ginny awoke at daybreak and looked to see if Emily was awake. When Emily stirred and opened her eyes, Ginny bent over her. "Would you like some breakfast, Emily?'' she asked. ''Look! Mommie has some cereal for you, and some milk.''

Understanding nothing, Emily got out of her sleeping bag and walked around the motel room, her face solemn and unsmiling.

Gently, Ginny took her hand.

''Look!'' she said in a loud whisper to the other Garths. ''Look, everybody! She's holding my hand. She likes me. Come, honey,'' she said to Emily. ''See! Mommie has some cereal for you. Um-m-m!'' She smacked her lips. ''Good cereal!''

Emily protested when Edie tried to lift her to a chair.

''You try lifting her, Ginny,'' suggested Edie.

''Look, honey,'' said Ginny, kneeling in front of Emily. ''I'm going to put you in this chair so you can eat your breakfast.''

This time Emily did not protest. She let Ginny lift her into the chair. When Ginny put a dish of cereal before her, she snatched the spoon and began shoveling the food into her mouth.

''The poor little thing is starved,'' said Julian.

''It must be really scary for her, being in a strange place and not understanding anything we say,'' said Ginny. ''I know I'd be scared.''

''Yeah,'' said Mark, ''I remember how it was.''

''She can't understand yet what we're saying,'' agreed Edie. ''But we can say things in such a way that she'll understand we love her. Ready to go?'' She held out her arms to lift Emily from the chair. But Emily fought her off.

''Let me try,'' said Ginny.

Ginny held out her arms. Emily went to her at once.

"Look!" said Ginny. "She thinks I'm her mother."

"I think we'll appoint you as her mother, Ginny," said Edie, "until she understands who we are and what we're saying to her."

With breakfast over, the Garths climbed into the minibus to drive home.

"The girls and Emily and I will sit in the middle seat," announced Edie. "You boys can sit in front with your father."

"That's not fair," complained Eric. "I want to sit with Emily."

"I do too," said Mark. "Why can't we take turns?"

"All right," agreed Edie. "When we've driven fifty miles, we'll change seats. You boys may sit back here with Emily, and the girls may sit up front with their father."

That being agreed on, with everyone partly happy, partly unhappy, they started out, watching the odometer. Emily refused to sit on the seat or on Edie's lap or on Ginny's. Again she stood solemnly holding to the back of the front seat.

"Why is she so sad?" asked Angela.

"Perhaps we'll never know," Edie told her. "We'll just have to be patient till we can make her happy. After awhile she'll get used to us and will understand she needn't be sad anymore."

At the end of fifty miles, Eric and Mark exchanged seats with Angela and Ginny. But Emily had no more to do with them than with the girls. She stood holding to the back of the front seat, her small face anxious, her eyes afraid.

Once in awhile Mark reached forward and touched her arm gently. After a time he announced, "When I get married, I'm going to adopt some children."

"I'm going to adopt ten," announced Angela from the front seat.

"Humph!" snorted Mark. "I'm going to adopt lots more than that. I'm going to adopt twenty."

"Ten," said Angela.

"Twenty," said Mark.

"Where would twenty children sleep?" asked Edie.

"Some could sleep on the roof," said Mark. "Some could sleep with me. And some could sleep on the floor."

"Why would you like so many, Mark?" asked Edie.

"Because," said Mark, "if you fight, and you need a lot of help, you can get a lot of help. And there are a lot of jobs to be done, so there would be plenty of kids to get all the jobs done."

"Another thing," said Angela, "if you have a big family, and if you don't know anybody in the neighborhood and nobody knows you, and you don't have any friends, well, you always have somebody to play with."

"There's one thing though," said Ginny. "If there aren't so many kids in the family, you can have more friends sleep overnight. And that's fun."

"But if you have just a few kids," said Mark, "and they're different colors, people passing by stare at you."

"That's because they think we're pretty," said Angela.

"It's because they think, how can that be? Parents having different kinds of kids?" said Mark. "And I'd like to say to them, 'They adopted us. And what's wrong with having different kinds of kids? And what's the matter with being adopted?' ''

"Do you know what adopted means, Mark?" asked Julian.

"It means forever and forever," said Mark. "It means somebody cares about you. And the kids get the jobs done."

"Honey," Ginny turned to Emily, still solemnly clutching the back of the front seat, "how do you like being adopted? Don't you think it's super?"

Emily stared ahead, unsmiling.

When finally the Garths reached home, Angela ran to bring Gene, Peter, and Julie from the Donaldsons'. All four came running home, falling over one another to get into the house first, and shouting, "Where's Emily? I want to see Emily!"

"Sh-h-h!" Ginny put her finger to her lips to silence them. "You'll scare her, shouting that way."

Shyly, for a moment, the children stared at Emily. Then, Peter walked to her and gently took her hand. Emily, frightened, pulled away.

"Why is she like that, Mommie?" asked Peter.

"She won't talk to us or anything," complained Gene.

"She can't talk to you yet, Gene," explained Edie. "The words she knows are different from ours. If she talked, you wouldn't understand anything she said. None of us would understand. We have to be patient and teach her our words."

"She won't even smile," complained Gene.

"One day she'll smile," promised Edie. "On the day she's happy, she'll smile."

"Will she be unhappy a long time?" asked Peter.

"We hope not," said Edie.

The rest of the day, Emily clung to Ginny. It was Ginny who must sit beside her at the table, Ginny who must hold her hand when they went outdoors, Ginny who must get her ready for bed. The next morning it was Ginny who must help her dress.

"All the time Ginny," complained Gene, on the verge of tears. "You be Emily's mother. You never play with me anymore."

"Listen, Gene," said Ginny. "You're a big boy now, see?"

"I'm not much bigger than Emily," said Gene.

"But you've been a Garth a lot longer," Ginny reminded him. "That means you're big enough to help somebody else. And whatever else it means, it means you're too big to be babied anymore. You see if you can't stand on your own two feet now. I'll just bet you can."

When breakfast was finished, Eric, Ginny, Angela, and Mark started off to school. At sight of Ginny leaving, Emily burst into loud, forlorn crying.

For a minute, Gene watched and listened. Then, taking Emily's hand, he said soothingly, "Don't cry, Emily. Ginny'll come back. While she's gone I'll be your mother."

Emily let him hold her hand. After a time her sobs subsided. Gene lifted the bottom of her dress and wiped her eyes.

"She thinks I'm her mother," Gene whispered to Edie.

"Want to come outdoors and play?" he asked. "With Julie and Peter and me?"

Solemnly Emily let herself be led into the big backyard.

"We'll catch bugs and worms and things," Gene promised. "You'll like that."

For weeks, into vacation time, Emily crammed into her mouth every scrap of food Edie put on her plate, and held her plate for more. She grew. She followed the other children around, always close to Ginny, but she never said a word, either in English or in Vietnamese. And never once did she smile.

On a sunny Saturday morning, soon after their chores were finished, all the children were busy in the backyard. Angela and Julie were playing with their dolls in the tree house Julian had built for them. Eric, sitting on the ground with his back propped against a tree, was reading a book. Mark, followed by Gene and Peter, was on the far bank of the creek, hot on the trail of a high-jumping frog. Ginny was swinging Emily in the rope swing.

"Look how high I'm swinging Emily!" called Ginny. "Look, everybody!"

All the children looked.

Emily was swinging so high that her toes were almost touching the low branches of the tree.

"Hey!" shouted Eric excitedly, throwing his book aside and jumping to his feet. "Look at Emily! Look at her! Everybody, look!"

All the Garths quit what they were doing, and looked. Then, leaving Emily swinging, in one wild scramble they raced into the house, Angela turning cartwheels in her excitement.

"Mommie! Mommie!" they shouted, each trying to outshout the others.

"It's happened! It's happened! Emily smiled! Everything's all right now! She smiled! She really did!"

The front door opened and Julian walked in.

"Daddy!" the shouting started again. "Emily smiled!"

Edie looked down at Mark and Gene and Peter. "Boys!" she scolded. "What in the world have you been doing? You're soaked to your knees. Shoes and all."

"Mommie," said Julian, smiling, "don't you know the quickest way to cross a creek when you're bursting with good news?"

Before the boys could explain, the back door was softly pushed open. In the doorway stood Emily. The smile was still on her face.

REBECCA CAUDILL is the author of many well-loved books for children. A number of them, including *A Certain Small Shepherd, Did You Carry the Flag Today, Charley?* and *A Pocketful of Cricket,* are set in Harlan County, Kentucky, where she was born and lived as a small child before moving to Tennessee. A sensitive observer, Miss Caudill draws her books from what she sees and feels around her, as well as from memories of her own childhood. *Somebody Go and Bang a Drum* is closely based on a real family.

The author has been honored many times by universities and organizations for her outstanding contribution to children's literature, and there is a Rebecca Caudill Library in Cumberland, Kentucky. Miss Caudill and her husband, the author James Ayars, live in Urbana, Illinois.